PRAISE FOR THE HOWARD

★“. . . . an absolute delight, told with clear affection for the usual P.I. story tropes and injecting them with just the right amount of amusement while avoiding sarcastic mockery.” —***BULLETIN OF THE CENTER FOR CHILDREN’S BOOKS*** **(STARRED REVIEW)**

“Strong writing, relatable themes, and a solid mystery combine for a read that both boys and girls will have trouble putting down.” —**SCHOOL LIBRARY JOURNAL**

“Give this to fans of Encyclopedia Brown who are looking for longer (and funnier!) well-plotted mysteries.” —**BOOKLIST**

“Lyall’s debut is a winner.” —**PUBLISHERS WEEKLY**

“Mystery fans should enjoy it . . . [it lands] in new territory, and the characters interact realistically and have real kid problems. —**KIRKUS REVIEWS**

HOWARD WALLACE, P.I.

SHADOW OF A PUG

by Casey Lyall

STERLING CHILDREN'S BOOKS
New York

STERLING CHILDREN'S BOOKS
New York

An Imprint of Sterling Publishing Co., Inc.
1166 Avenue of the Americas
New York, NY 10036

ISBN 978-1-4549-3260-4

Distributed in Canada by Sterling Publishing Co., Inc.
c/o Canadian Manda Group, 664 Annette Street
Toronto, Ontario M6S 2C8, Canada
Distributed in the United Kingdom by GMC Distribution Services
Castle Place, 166 High Street, Lewes, East Sussex BN7 1XU, England
Distributed in Australia by NewSouth Books
45 Beach Street, Coogee, NSW 2034, Australia

For information about custom editions, special sales, and premium and corporate purchases, please contact Sterling Special Sales at 800-805-5489 or specialsales@sterlingpublishing.com.

Manufactured in Canada

Lot #:
2 4 6 8 10 9 7 5 3 1
07/18

sterlingpublishing.com

Wallace and Mason Investigations

~~Mason and Wallace Investigations~~

Rules of Private Investigation

1. Work with what you've got. *Especially when it's a fabulous shade of green.*
2. Ask the right questions.
3. Know your surroundings.
4. Always have a cover story ready.
5. Blend in.
6. A bad plan is better than no plan. *I think we need to revisit this rule.* **No.**
7. Never underestimate your opponent.
8. Never tip your hand.
9. Don't get caught. *You should try following this rule, Howard.* **Stop it.**
10. Pick your battles.
11. Don't leave a trail.
12. Everyone has a hook.
13. *Always listen to your partner. She's a genius.*

Speaking of rules we need to revisit.

Very funny.

Chapter One

A bright light pierced my eyes, and they struggled to adjust. I caught flashes of the room around me: Bare walls. Scratched linoleum floor. The door slammed and my chair slowly tilted back. From the shadowy corner came a deep voice: "How many, Howard?"

"What?" I could barely make out the figure of a man.

He took a step closer. "You know what." A metal instrument glinted as he twisted it back and forth in his hands. "How many?"

Sweat burned a trail down my neck, and I squinted under the light. "Don't know what you're talking about."

A chair rolled across the floor, and Dr. Hunt came into

view, taking a seat in front of me. “How many packs of gum a day are you up to?”

Crossing my arms, I leaned back in my seat. “That’s a loaded question, Doc. Lemme ask you one first: What’s the cavity count?”

He slid over to the lightboard to pin up my x-rays. “Zero,” he mumbled, and I grinned. “But that doesn’t mean bad habits won’t catch up with you.”

“I floss.”

“It’s all a stopgap solution if you keep abusing your teeth this way.” Dr. Hunt passed me a small cup of fluoride, and I dutifully swished. I could tell him I’d tried to quit. Tried a million times, but the siren song of Juicy Smash kept pulling me back.

“I want you to cut back to one a day, understood?”

Empty promises weren’t my bag, but we’d done this dance before. There was one answer alone that would get me out of this chair. Fingers crossed, I nodded.

Dr. Hunt smiled, relief plain across his face as our semi-annual ordeal came to a close. He pointed at the cup in my hand.

“Now, spit.”

-. .. -.-. -.- .- -. -.. -. --- .-. .-

An hour later, freshly polished teeth and all, I was on my way downtown to meet up with my partner, Ivy Mason. We held check-ins every Friday afternoon at Mrs. Hernandez's bakery—case updates with a side of donut. It was a win-win.

I'd nearly reached the door of the shop when it flew open and a small figure barreled past. "Watch it!" I yelled after him. The blurry shape of Ivy streaked by next, successfully sending me to the pavement. "What's happening?"

"Thief!" Ivy yelled back at me. "Chase! Come on, Howard Wallace!" I scrambled to my feet and took off after them.

There were only so many places to run in Grantleyville, and our suspect seemed determined to hit them all before we caught up to him. One left turn followed another. Pretty soon we'd made a full circuit around the main drag. My partner and I pounded down the sidewalk in hot pursuit, our heels sinking in the mid-February slush.

"Hurry up, Howard," Ivy called. "We've almost got him!" She surged ahead and followed the perp down a side street. Tightening up my lucky coat, I chased after them.

Unfortunately, I still wasn't fast enough.

A crash rang out as I rounded the corner and was brought up short by a pile of arms and legs rolling around on the ground. "Ivy," I said, panting. "We talked about this. Tackling is never the answer."

The mess of limbs sorted themselves out. Ivy emerged, sitting on top of the kid, pinning him to the ground. "But it works so well," she said, grinning.

"What'd he do?"

"Stole Mrs. Hernandez's purse. Went right behind the counter, then took off. Little punk."

Taking a closer look at his face, I sighed. I actually knew this particular punk—as did Grantleyville's Finest. I crouched down beside the poor twerp who was getting an asphalt facial. "Toby," I said. "Let's talk about your choices. Petty crime being what led you here, and fessing up being your only way out."

"What?" Eleven years of living hadn't done much for Toby's listening comprehension skills.

"Give us the bag, Toby," I said. "I bet Mrs. Hernandez is willing to take it easy on you."

"Ooh, slight problem with that, partner," Ivy said. "He ditched the goods."

I shook my head. "Where?"

She jerked a nod over her shoulder. "Dumpster."

"What'd you go and do that for?"

"Think I'm an idiot?" Toby said, struggling under Ivy. He curled his lip at me. "Evasive maneuvers. Trying not to get caught."

"Didn't really work out, did it? Next time don't swipe a purse in front of a double-A-plus detective," Ivy said.

"Let him up," I said. "We have to figure out how we're getting that bag back."

She hopped off Toby, brushing the dirt from her pants. He quickly followed suit. I pulled a pack of Juicy out of my pocket and popped a piece.

"I thought you quit," Ivy said, holding out a hand.

"I did." Tossing her the pack, I snapped a bubble in my mouth. "Yesterday."

"Bet Dr. Hunt was pleased."

"Gave me three toothbrushes," I said. I reached out and hauled Toby back by the collar to stop his inching escape. "We're not done with you. Let's talk."

Ivy and I faced off against our perp, hitting him with a double-edged glare. "What were you thinking?" I asked. "Stealing Mrs. Hernandez's bag like that?"

"My sister dared me," he said, puffing out his chest like a tiny, scraggly haired chipmunk. "She didn't think I could do it." Toby was a Turner, a clan as extensive and entitled as the town's namesake, the Grantleys, but without the wealth to wipe away their crimes. The Turners had their own heading in the misdemeanors section of the *Grantleyville Herald.* A kid like Toby started out small change, working his way up in the family business.

Ivy and I exchanged a look. Turning him in wasn't going to do him any favors. "Stay here," I said. "You know we'll catch you again if you bolt."

He scoffed. "Like I'm afraid of a kid in a bathrobe."

I held out the sides of my lucky coat, half-hidden by the winter coat that Ma made me throw on over it. "In detective circles, this is what's known as a trench coat," I said. "And if you run, Ivy'll just tackle you again."

Ivy nodded enthusiastically.

Toby deflated a bit, walking over to stand by the fence backing the alley. I took it as acceptance of his fate. A quick examination of the dumpster told me this wasn't going to be pretty. Ivy gave it a kick. "Who's going in?"

"You should go in," I said. "You're the one who watched him toss it."

"We would have caught him sooner if you hadn't been such a slowpoke."

"Should we settle this like professionals?" I rolled up my sleeves.

"On three," Ivy agreed.

"Wait, on three, or one, two, three, go?"

"You do this every time," Ivy said. "One, two, three, go would be 'on four.' On three is on three."

"I'm merely trying to make sure we're on the same page here," I said.

"You're trying to psych me out so you win, and it ain't happening, Howard Wallace," she said. "I know all your tricks. Now. On three."

"One, two . . ." I said, then hit my fist in my hand, two fingers out. "Oh, man."

"Ahaha!" Ivy crowed. "Rock crushes scissors. Get in there, friend."

I climbed up the side of the dumpster and peered over the edge. My head began to swim. Heights and I were not close friends, and clinging to the side of the bin wasn't helping matters. It looked less than inviting. Smelled even worse. Unseasonably warm weather had melted the snow piled inside, resulting in a sludge dotted with garbage-bag dumplings. Bits of loose debris bubbled up to drift lazily around the cesspool of junk. On the far side, perched on a tiny mountain of dry bags, was the purse. It was going to survive this ordeal in better shape than whoever went to retrieve it.

A particularly strong whiff of the potent concoction cleared my head enough for a genius idea to pop through.

Hopping off the dumpster, I trotted over to where Toby was shivering by the fence. I should probably have felt worse about what I was about to do, but there was a reason they called it learning the hard way. "Up and at 'em, Toby," I said. "You're going in."

"Me?" Toby blinked. "In there?"

"Howard," Ivy hissed behind me, "what are you doing?"

"We're teaching him about consequences," I said. "Now, Toby, it was your bright idea to steal the bag and then dump it, so it seems fair to me you retrieve it."

"Yeah, I don't think so," Toby said. "I'm good right here."

"Let me spell out your options." I stomped my feet against the wind picking up down the alley. "One, we leave the bag there and call the cops to deal with the both of you."

"Fine by me," he said with a sneer that left me tempted to follow through on option one.

In the spirit of education, I carried on. "Of course, when

the police come, everyone will find out you got busted by a couple of seventh-grade detectives—"

"*Awesome* seventh-grade detectives, and one did more busting than the other," Ivy interjected.

I raised an eyebrow and she motioned for me to continue. "Something tells me that situation won't win you any points with the family," I said. "Option number two is we settle this quietly. You grab the bag, give it back to Mrs. H, apologize—"

"Sincerely." Ivy waggled a finger at him.

"—you'll owe us a favor, and the whole thing is settled. Take your time. Mull."

Ivy pulled on my sleeve and motioned me over. "He'll owe us a favor?"

"Seemed like a good idea to tack on," I said.

"I thought we were trying to steer him away from trouble."

"First rule of private investigation, Ivy?"

She screwed up her nose, keeping one eye on our perp. "How does 'work with what you've got' apply here?"

"Every P.I. worth their salt has a thief on tap," I said. "Gotta build up the resources."

"It makes a bizarre sort of sense," Ivy said. She pulled her hat down over her ears and sighed. "Carry on."

We looked over at Toby. "Time's up," I said. "What'll it be?"

He muttered an answer and I cupped my ear. "Speak up, young offender."

"Option number two," he snapped, dragging his feet over to the bin. We boosted him up, stepping back as he landed with a plop. After a moment of silence, his voice drifted over. "It's really gross in here."

"Think about this moment next time you try your hand at petty crime," I called out. We listened to him squidge his way over to the purse.

"Heads up."

Ivy caught the bag as it went whizzing by. "Got it."

Toby's head emerged over the side. "Are you guys going to help me out of here?"

"Let me see your hands," I said.

He held up garbage-free mitts, and we each grabbed one to yank him out, leaping back as his pants left a trail of muck along the ground.

"This is going back to Mrs. H," Ivy said, tucking the purse under her arm. She held up a finger to test the wind before pointing at Toby. "And *you* are going to walk ten feet ahead of us. Try not to drip."

We marched him back around the corner to Mrs. Hernandez's coffee shop. With some less-than-gentle prodding, he offered his apology, and she accepted. Mostly she was overjoyed to see her belongings returned intact. "Thank you so much! What do I owe you?" she asked Ivy and me.

"It was a case of right place at the right time." My partner waved her off. "I couldn't stand by while someone pulled a lift right in front of me."

"Well, I appreciate it," Mrs. Hernandez said before disappearing into the back. She returned with a white envelope in hand, sliding it across the counter. "Consider this a bonus." I peeked inside. Cold, hard cash: my favorite kind of payment. Ivy rolled her eyes as I pocketed the envelope.

"What?" I grinned. "I helped. Partners share, right?"

"I'm taking a tackling bonus out of there," Ivy said.

"I should get a tackling bonus," Toby grumbled.

"Crime doesn't pay, Toby," I shook my head. "Crime doesn't pay."

Mrs. Hernandez smirked. "I'm going to take Toby into the back to discuss compensation for what he's put me through today. I think we'll start with mopping up whatever it is you trailed in here, yeah?" She skated a glass dish over toward me and Ivy. "Help yourself to some treats before you go."

A cookie in each hand, Ivy and I wandered back to my

neighborhood. "Being paid in baked goods isn't half bad," she said between bites. "We should incorporate that into our fee structure."

"It's not bad, but I prefer money," I said, tapping the envelope in my pocket. "I'll take a wad of green over a handful of chocolate chips any day. Especially for such an easy job."

"Says the guy who didn't do any of the tackling."

"You don't get points for that," I said. "I've specifically asked you not to do that."

"I'm giving myself points," Ivy bounced down the sidewalk toward my house. "It was awesome." She stopped in her tracks to peer back at me. "This is the third case we've solved this week. Why aren't you more excited?"

Anyone's excitement paled next to Ivy's vibrating exuberance, but she wasn't wrong. I hadn't been feeling the usual post-case buzz lately. "They've all been open-and-shut cases. We haven't had a challenge since October." I smiled at the memory—a blackmail case that almost cost me my job and ended up saddling me and Ivy with multiple weeks of detention. Worth it. Kids were hiring us all the time now—and some adults, too.

"Weren't you the one who told me most of the jobs in a

town like Grantleyville were going to be boring? That a case like Meredith's was the exception and not the rule?"

I hated when she listened to what I said. "I don't think it's too much to ask for at least one to not be a total cakewalk." Each time we caught a new case, I hoped it'd be another doozy. The wait continued.

Ivy bumped my shoulder and the subject at hand. "Got your bag ready?" My parents had instituted "Date Night" a few months ago. Every other Friday they shipped me off to Ivy's and my sister, Eileen, to her best friend Angela's house. Previous attempts at leaving me in Eileen's care had proved disastrous.

"Yup," I said, perking up a bit. Maybe a crime wave would hit Grantleyville while we had movie night. A fella could dream.

Chapter Two

Ivy's grandma was waiting at the door when we arrived at her house.

"How's business?" she asked, tying a hot-pink apron around her waist.

"Messy," I said, toeing off my shoes and depositing my coat on the rack.

"It's about to get messier." She grinned at us. "Drop your stuff in the living room, and let's get going."

"What are we making tonight, Mrs. Mason?" I tossed my stuff onto the couch and wandered into the kitchen.

"Howard, for the last time, call me Lillian." She shook her head and tossed me my usual polka-dotted apron. "We're making breakfast for dinner. Pancakes are an eternal crowd-pleaser."

Mrs. Mason—Lillian—had decided from the get-go that we'd be in charge of our own Friday night meals. Apparently it was never too early to learn how to fend for yourself. Under her supervision, we'd only set off the smoke alarm twice.

Their kitchen was tiny and warm and more than a little bit crowded with the three of us huddled around the stove. Ivy and I both manned a burner, spatulas at the ready. After a few failed attempts, I was on the road to mastering the perfect flip, acquiring a small stack of flawlessly round and fluffy pancakes.

Ivy had taken an alternate approach.

Glancing over at her pan, I squinted. "What's that one?"

"Pterodactyl," she said, frowning in concentration as she lifted it onto her stack of odd, semiburned shapes.

Glad I didn't voice my guess of a palm tree.

"Is that breakfast for dinner I smell?" Ivy's dad poked his head into the kitchen. "My favorite." He wandered into the room, one hand rubbing at tired eyes behind his wire-rimmed glasses.

"Have a seat," Ivy said, pointing at the small, round table in the corner. "We're just about ready."

"Sorry, sweetie," he said. "I'm eating at my desk tonight. Too many files to go through."

Ivy and her grandma shared a sigh. "Tax season."

"Hi, Howard." Mr. Mason grabbed a plate, scooping a few

pancakes off Ivy's pile. He pointed at the top one. "Pterodactyl?" He nodded at Ivy's grin. "Nice."

"Take orange juice," Lillian called after his retreating form. "Man thinks he can live on coffee alone."

"It's brain juice," Mr. Mason said over his shoulder.

The rest of us gathered our plates and sat around the tiny kitchen table. Ivy was quiet, stealing glances down the hall toward her dad's office.

"What's on the agenda for tonight?" Lillian asked.

"The usual," I said. "Movies. Eating."

"We're going to work on our marketing strategies too," Ivy piped up. "Try to snag some new cases."

"If you really want to get some good ideas," Lillian said. "You've got to start thinking outside the box. Sam Spade is fine, but not every detective is a smirk in a trench coat. There are other ways to do things."

I inhaled the rest of my perfectly fluffy pancakes. "What are you suggesting?"

"Time to add another chapter to your training regime." Lillian winked.

-. .. -.-. -.-   .- -. -..   -. --- .-. .-

After the dishes were done and the kitchen tidied up, Lillian clapped her hands together. "Ready to get started?"

"Just one second," Ivy said, pulling a glass out of the cupboard. "I'll meet you in the living room." She filled the cup with orange juice and hurried down the hall.

Lillian and I arranged the living room, and I was all snuggled into the comfy end of the couch when Ivy came in. She stopped short at the sight of me. "That's my spot."

"You snooze, you lose," I said.

Ivy narrowed her eyes, then cut a smile that had my own smirk falling off my face. She was airborne before I had a chance to move an inch.

"Ooof." Ivy landed on top of me, squishing me deep into the cushions. "No tackling," I said weakly while she cackled.

"Settle down, shenaniganizers," Lillian tutted. "That couch is on its last legs."

We untangled and somehow Ivy managed to end up back in "her" spot. "That was a dirty trick," I grumbled.

"It was the couch, I swear." Ivy held her hands up. "I can't help it if it loves me more."

"Hush, the lot of you," Lillian said. "Prepare yourselves to be amazed and entertained." She pressed Play and sat back on the couch as the show began.

"Tiny little town," Ivy said, watching the scenery unfold. "It could be Grantleyville."

"This lady doesn't look like much of a detective." I eyed the tidy-looking woman on the screen.

"That's Jessica. She's a writer," Ivy's grandma said. "It's an entirely different dress code."

"Oh, don't go in there," Ivy said. "You never find anything good in creepy, old houses."

"Go in the house," I cheered. "Go in the house!"

"I need popcorn for this," Lillian said, boosting herself up off the couch and heading for the kitchen. Ivy and I continued watching *Murder, She Wrote,* dissecting all the clues as they cropped up.

Ivy's grandma returned with a huge bowl of popcorn. "What'd I miss?"

"Jessica's found *two* bodies already," I said. "Cabot Cove is way more exciting than Grantleyville."

"I don't think we need that much excitement here, Howard," Ivy said, leaning back and tossing popcorn into her mouth.

"Speak for yourself," I muttered.

Lillian sat through three episodes with us before raising her arms up in a stretch. "These old bones are going to bed," she said over the sound of joints popping and cracking. "'Night, kids. Don't stay up too late."

"'Night, Lillian," I said. Ivy hugged her grandma good-night. We settled into our sleeping bags as the show continued and the body count continued to climb.

"Okay, seriously," Ivy said. "We're five episodes in, and that's how many murders? How is this town not on a watch list? Why does anyone still live there?"

"Because plot?" I flopped back onto my pillow. I was more than a little envious of Jessica's caseload. Not that I wanted us to be stumbling across a murder scene in a creepy old house. But if we did, Ivy and I could handle it. Maybe. Probably.

Ivy paused the show. "Talk."

"What?"

"You're thinking so loud, I can hear you over the TV."

"I was just thinking: Grantleyville could do with a little plot," I said, sitting up.

My partner nodded, her face growing serious. "I agree." She reached behind her back and whipped her pillow out, hitting me full-on with a giant *whump.* I fell back on to the floor, stunned.

"Oh, man," she said. "I think I just stumbled across a body in the living room. Hang on. Lemme check." She smacked me again with the pillow. "Yup, definitely dead."

"Check again." I grabbed my own pillow and returned fire. Ivy's eyes widened as she cackled. Our sleeping bags were kicked to the side as the pillow fight escalated into a pillow war.

"Ahem."

I paused midswing at the voice coming from the doorway. Ivy's dad leaned against the wall, eyebrows raised. "Having a restful evening, are we?"

Ivy and I stammered out apologies as he grinned. "If I can hear you in my office, it's only a matter of time before your grandma gets woken up," he said. "And trust me, you don't want her coming in here next."

"Sorry, Dad," Ivy said. "We'll be quiet."

"'Night, kids."

We set our sleeping bags out again as he left, and I flipped off the living room light. Ivy turned off the TV before stretching out on the floor. I started to relax, listening to Ivy's breathing evening out beside me.

"For the record," I whispered. "I was winning." The room was silent as I waited for Ivy's response.

"Go to sleep, Howard," she said.

It was too dark for her to see my smirk, but she heard it loud and clear. I barely heard a rustle before the pillow came out of nowhere and bopped my face.

"'Night, Ivy."

Chapter Three

Sleep had been hard won after a night of popcorn and small-town murder. Lying on the floor in a sleeping bag wasn't optimal either. The luxury of sleeping in slowly slipped through my grasp as I surfaced to the most annoying sound in the world.

"Howard. Howard. Howard. *Howard.*" Ivy was chanting my name with a fair amount of glee in her voice. I could feel a twitch building between my eyes. I opened them to see her staring at me, her nose barely an inch away from mine.

"Oh, good," she said. "You're awake."

"The question is, why?"

"We have a million things to do today and we're already late."

"Saturday," I groaned.

"Yup," Ivy said. "Chore time."

The only downside of our Friday night sleepovers: Ivy had managed to wrangle me into helping her with her list of Saturday chores after the first night. Since then, it had somehow become part of our routine. We grabbed a bowl of cereal before putting the living room back in order and tackling the laundry. Ivy's house was quiet. Her grandma volunteered at the library on Saturdays, and her dad was already back in his office. After vacuuming and tidying up the kitchen, Ivy and I flopped back onto the couch, putting our feet up on the coffee table.

"That's it," Ivy said. "I'm done-zo."

"I hate to break it to you, partner, but we still have one more job."

"But the list," Ivy whimpered. "We crossed off all the things."

"For your house," I said. "Pops wants us to tidy up the garage. He says the office is starting to spread." I hauled myself up off the couch and held out a hand. Ivy took it, pulling herself up to her feet.

"Okay, fine," she said. "Anything for Pops."

I grabbed my bag and we bundled up before heading outside. Ivy hopped along the sidewalk beside me, her mood picking up as she breathed in the fresh air.

"Hey." She poked me with an elbow. "What do you think about advertising?"

"In the general sense?"

"In the 'for our business' sense," she said. "We mostly go on word of mouth, but maybe if we put in some effort, we'd attract bigger cases."

"What are you thinking?"

"I don't know. Posters, maybe? Something online?"

I mulled it over. "That's actually not a bad idea."

"Of course it's not," Ivy said. "That's why I'm your partner. You'd be lost without me."

I elbowed her back and she laughed. We spent the rest of the trip to my house discussing slogans and color schemes for possible ads.

"I bet you Mrs. Hernandez would let us put one up in her shop," I said as we walked up my driveway.

"There you are." My mother poked her head out the side door. "Have you eaten?"

"We had some cereal earlier, Mrs. Wallace," Ivy said.

"Come on in and have a snack before you take on the office." She disappeared back inside, and we followed. I tossed my bag onto the floor and hung up my coat by the door.

"I know that thump was the sound of you putting your bag away properly," Ma called from the kitchen.

Ivy snickered at me as I picked up my bag from the floor and carried it up to my room. My partner was seated at the kitchen table when I came back, munching on apple slices.

"How was your night?" Ma asked as she set a plate in front of me.

"Good," I said. "How was Date Night?"

"Good," she said with a smile that made me regret asking. "What are your plans for the day?"

"Office," I said. "And then working on a new business plan."

"Full schedule then," Ma said. She set a container of cookies on the table.

Ivy nodded enthusiastically, grabbing a cookie and tossing one to me. "We should probably take some of these with us to keep our energy up."

We all jumped as feet thundered down the stairs and Eileen burst into the kitchen. "Where have you been?"

"At Ivy's," I said, leaning back to take a leisurely bite of my cookie. "Why? Did you miss me?"

Eileen shot me a look. She hadn't missed my presence since I learned how to talk. "Marvin's called you like six hundred times, and I'm trying to study. I don't have time for—"

"What'd he want?" I cut in before she could get on a roll.

"I believe the words you're looking for are 'thank you,' Howard," my mother cut in.

"Thank you, Eileen," I said. "What'd he want?"

"I'm not your lackey, Howeird," she said, shoving a piece of paper into my hand. "I have better things to do with my time."

"And the words you're looking for, Eileen, are 'you're welcome,' " Ma said with a sigh.

"You're welcome," Eileen snapped. "Put me on the payroll if you want me to keep taking your messages."

"Cookie?" I held out one of Ma's magical chocolate-chip concoctions. "You can eat around the bite."

She turned her nose up at my offered payment before spotting the full container on the table. Grabbing it, she stalked back down the hall, fuming about her current living conditions before stomping up the stairs. Her bedroom door slammed moments later. Girl knew how to make an exit. Uncrumpling the note, I barely had time to decipher Eileen's scrawl before Ivy snatched it out of my hands.

My partner scanned the message, and a slow grin took over her face as she said our four favorite words:

"We have a case."

Chapter Four

"Do you think it's a real job, or are we gonna end up cleaning out his storage room again?" Ivy looked back as she leapt nimbly over the rivers of melted snow running down the sidewalk. "Because that was disgusting and once was enough."

"He actually said *case* this time, so the odds are good it's legit." I splashed along behind her, wishing my ride was here to save me from the treacherous terrain ahead, but Blue was useless in this kind of weather. My ancient bike had a strict hibernation policy. She holed up in our garage from the first frost until at least the beginning of April. That left me hoofing it all winter long.

Marvin helped us out of a couple of jams a few months

back, including our big blackmail case. Since he preferred to remain off the books, he took his fee in favors. After he'd called in the first one, it became clear that failing to negotiate the parameters of the favors was a mistake. However, a deal was a deal, and at Wallace and Mason Investigations, our word was our bond. Even if that word led us to cleaning out a room full of junk Marvin's customers wouldn't touch with a ten-foot pole.

We arrived at the fractured steps of Marvin's on Main. Ivy sprinted ahead to be first through the door. She'd only been there a few times, but after the first visit she'd declared the pawnshop "one of the top five places to be in Grantleyville." I'd been afraid to ask what the other four were.

The bell on the door clanked softly as we entered, years of dust muting whatever chimes it had once possessed. "Marvin," I called out. "We're here."

"In the back," came the gravelly reply.

"Ivy—" I turned to find an empty space where my partner had been, and bit back a growl. "Ivy."

She leapt out from behind the next set of shelves, decked out in a fringed vest and a gardening hat, carrying a blue guitar. "Yes?" The hat flopped down, and she shoved it up with an arm covered in about a dozen bracelets.

"Ivy, cool it. We're working," I said. "Paws off the merchandise."

"I can't help myself," she said, strumming tunelessly on the guitar. "This store is awesome."

"I'm not getting any younger over here," Marvin hollered from the back.

"Understatement of the year," Ivy whispered. I shot her a look as she mugged. "I'm putting it away, relax." She tossed the hat and guitar up on a shelf and slid the bracelets onto the counter. "You have to admit: I'm totally pulling this off," she said, swishing the fringe of her vest at me.

"Yeah, you're a regular fashion plate," Marv said, shuffling through the doorway, spindly arms wrapped up in a moth-eaten brown sweater. "If you solve my case, you can keep it."

"Really?" Ivy beamed.

"No." He pushed us down the hallway into the kitchenette. "Get in here so I can tell you about this job before I die."

We were escorted into a tiny room decked out in yellowed wallpaper whose design had long since become one with the cobwebs. Mugs littered the counter, and the faint scent of burnt coffee hung in the air. Marvin pulled out a plastic lawn chair, sending the papers piled on it tumbling to the floor.

"Take a seat," he said. "We gotta lot of ground to cover and you took your sweet time getting here."

Ivy and I sat gingerly on either side of the chair. It looked like it had last been cleaned around the same time as the walls. "We were working a case," I said. "Things got messy."

"I heard." Marvin wheezed. "Mrs. H has that little delinquent cleaning her shop from top to bottom." News traveled fast in a town this size.

"We're more interested in hearing about your case," Ivy said. "What's up?"

"I've got a real humdinger for you." He rubbed at his chin and frowned. "My nephew's got himself in a spot of trouble."

"Nephew?" Given Marvin's indecipherable age, it was hard to gauge how old this nephew could be. The spectrum of trouble we were looking at was potentially vast.

"Grandnephew," he clarified. "My little sister's grandson. He's about your age."

"What's the trouble?"

"He's taking the fall for some ridiculous prank over at the school, and it sounds like a suspension is the least of our worries." Marvin grunted his opinion on the matter. "I need you to help clear his name."

"That's a pretty big case, Marvin," I said. "We talking clean slate after this?"

"Wiped clean until the next favor."

Ivy whipped out her notebook and held a pen at the ready. "Give us the details. Who's your nephew?"

Marvin craned his head to look out the doorway, peering blearily through the smeared lenses of his glasses. "I told him to come by. He's late as usual." On cue, the front door opened, the bell clunking at the arrival of our new client.

"Uncle Marv?" a voice called out.

A familiar voice.

Ivy caught my eye, and I could see the same question on her face.

Footsteps came down the hallway as recognition began to dawn.

Of course I knew that voice. It lived in my nightmares and plagued my days.

It belonged to my third-worst enemy.

The one and only Carl Dean.

Chapter Five

A shocked silence reigned as Carl walked into the miniscule kitchen. He stopped short at the sight of us at the table. I was still cursing Marvin's family tree when Carl found his voice.

"Uncle Marv?"

"Well, nice talking to you, Marvin, but there's no way this is happening," I said, pushing away from the table. I stuffed my notebook back in my pocket and jabbed a pen in Carl's direction. "You're going to have to pick a new way to cash in your favor. I don't work with cretins."

"Careful, Howard," Marvin said. "We all have our faults."

Ivy snorted. "Some more than others." We both glared at Carl, and he stared back, impassive face unreadable as usual.

He was like a brick wall: hard, wide, and impossible to tell what was going on beyond it. I'd seen a few sparks of character during our big blackmail case, but it'd been business as usual since then. Business being violence against my person and the thieving of my belongings.

"I'm with Howard on this one," Ivy said, arms crossed, face set. "There are limits."

"I'm sorry, Marv," I said. "I'll honor our deal, but not like this. Not for him." Ivy and I headed toward the door when Marvin's voice stopped me in my tracks.

"So, that's how it is? The great detective gives his word and then walks away?"

Doubt and resentment battled in my chest. Throwing my own code back in my face was a low blow and Marvin knew it. He held up his hands, waiting for me to respond, a glimmer in his eye daring me to say no. Professional integrity or pride? This was a lose-lose situation.

"Howard," Ivy said, standing in front of me and grabbing the sleeves of my coat, "this idiot has stolen from you, beaten you up, and given you wedgies. He's not worthy of our help."

Marvin sat up in his chair, a phlegmy cough rumbling in his agitation. "Carl, what are they talking about? You messed with these guys?"

He shrugged, scuffing the floor with his shoe. "Mostly Tim did."

Marvin turned to us. "Now that kid is a cretin." No one argued with that. Tim was Carl's partner-in-crime. They used their eighth-grade clout and general overgrown-ness to pursue illicit gain—activities that had helped bump Tim up to number two on my list of adversaries. He was also a Grantley, although he swam in the shallower end of their gene pool. The fact remained: Tim was rich enough to buy himself and his friends out of any kind of trouble they cooked up . . . and he did. Frequently. The need for this meeting was beginning to perplex me.

"Why isn't he helping you out?" I asked Carl.

"Yes." Ivy jumped all over that option. "Call Tim. Problem solved."

Carl's ears pinked up, and he studied the ceiling.

"About that . . ." Marvin pulled a stained handkerchief from his pocket and unloaded both barrels into it, one nostril after the other. If this was the prep work, I could hardly wait for the explanation. "Tim's out of the picture." He shrugged, and curiosity got the better of Ivy.

"What do you mean 'out of the picture'?" she asked.

"Kid's happy to be a delinquent as long as there are no

consequences," Marvin said, swiping at the table with his hankie before pocketing it. "One whiff of real trouble and he turned tail. Never mind the fact that Carl didn't do anything. School started talking suspension, and he was out. Too afraid of what Daddy will say to stick around."

"Nice friends you got there," I said. "Leaving you twisting in the wind."

The twitching muscle in Carl's jaw was the only acknowledgment that he'd heard that statement.

Ivy clapped her hands together, returning to her senses. "Still don't see how it's our problem."

"What can they do, anyway?" Carl said, slouching against the wall.

"You know exactly what we can do, Carl," I snapped. "Let's not pretend otherwise. Better think twice about how you talk, if you want our help."

Ivy crossed her arms, doubling down on my glare. "Which you're not getting anyway."

Marvin smacked a fist down on the table, silencing the room. "I don't care about whatever beef is between you. Howard, we had a deal. You owe me a favor and I'm calling it in. We need your help on this. That's all there is to it."

Carl, Ivy, and I stared at each other for a moment. This

was my own fault for griping about easy cases. "I need to talk to my partner," I said. Ivy and I legged it out into the hallway and holed up in the storage room. Even after our cleaning session, it barely had enough room for the two of us.

Ivy flopped down onto a crate, her mouth set in a mutinous line. "We're not taking the case, Howard. I don't care what Marvin says."

"Trust me, I'm not happy about this either," I said. "If I could walk us out of here, I would. Whatever trouble Carl's in, I'm sure he earned it."

"So what's the problem? We tell them no deal."

The problem.

I scrubbed a hand over my face and motioned for her to move over. Reason was knocking on the door frustration had slammed shut. Grabbing a seat beside Ivy, I sighed. I was already regretting my next words. "The problem is, Marvin's right. We owe him. If we walk away from that, our name will be mud. No one's gonna want to hire P.I.s who don't keep their word."

"Even if the client's nephew is a jerk."

"Yes," I said. "Even if the client's nephew is a no-good, snack-stealing, bike-mocking, head-busting, jerk-faced jerk."

"We heard that," Marvin called out.

"Good!" Ivy and I shouted.

My partner kicked her heels against the crate, grumbling. "This is so dumb. You know, you could be trying a little harder to figure a way out of this mess."

I tipped my hat back on my head. "I'm all ears, sweetheart, if you've got any bright ideas."

"Don't get all Bogart on me," she snapped. "This is serious!"

"Believe me, I know," I said. "You think I want to be stuck working with that pile of muscles? Not a chance." I tugged on the end of Ivy's scarf until she looked up to meet my eyes. "But if we walk out on Marvin, he'll be peeved enough to go yapping around town, and then where will we be?"

I took my partner's silence as begrudging concession. "It could be worse."

She considered that while she sulked. "How?"

"His nephew could have been Tim."

"You're not even a little bit funny," Ivy said, chuckling despite herself. Her laughter faded out into a sigh. "We're taking this case, aren't we?"

"We're probably taking this case."

"Howard . . ." She drew my name out as she buried her face in her hands.

"We need to at least hear their story," I said. "And by *them* I mean Marvin."

"Ugh." Ivy hauled herself up off the crate and pointed a finger at me. "After this, no more favors. We're going strictly on the books."

"Fair enough," I said.

We walked back to the kitchen, taking our time before facing the task ahead. Marvin and Carl were seated at the table when we entered, heads close together as they held a furious, whispered argument. They both sat back at the sight of us.

"Finally," Marvin said. "Took you long enough to come to your senses."

"We're not promising anything yet, Marv," I said. "Just hurry up and give us the details."

"Alright, alright," he said. "Keep your shirt on." Marvin nodded at Carl. "This one's been suspended from the basketball team, and they're talking about making it permanent if things don't get cleared up."

"What'd you do, Carl?"

"*I* didn't do anything." Carl tapped a nervous beat out on the table. "Coach accused me of stealing our mascot, but someone took him out of my yard."

I paused, pen hovering over my notebook. "I'm going to

need you to fill in some more blanks here, Carl. Who's the mascot, why'd you have it, and why would the coach think you'd steal it?"

He pulled up a picture on his phone and slid it across the table. Ivy and I leaned over to get a closer look.

"This doesn't clear anything up. Is that supposed to be a dog?" Between the bug eyes and squished nose, I wasn't entirely sure.

Carl snatched the phone back and held it tight. "It's a pug, and his name is Spartacus."

"You're kidding, right?"

"We're the Grantleyville Gladiators, so . . ."

"No, I get it. That's just a lot of name for a little dog."

"He's a good dog," Carl said, glowering at the picture. "Coach Williams has us all rotate turns taking care of him. Says it builds team spirit."

"So you had Spartacus and someone swiped him out of your yard?" Ivy looked up from her surprisingly accurate doodle of the doglet. "Where were you when this happened?"

"I went inside to get his ball, and when I came back he was gone. Our yard is fenced in; he didn't run away. Someone definitely took him."

"We're going to need to take a look at your yard," I said.

"Why does your coach think you had a hand in this? You explained what went down?"

"He wouldn't listen to me," Carl said. "He knows I've been mad 'cause he's had me riding the bench most of this season, but I'd never do anything to hurt Spartacus."

"Why aren't you playing?" Ivy tapped her pen against the table, frowning at Carl.

"There's a new crop of Grantleys on the team. Coach is a Grantley. Doesn't take a genius to do the math."

"Mr. Williams is a Grantley?" That was news to me.

"Barely," Marvin said. "Third or fourth cousin. Nowhere near the inner circle. He's always sucking up to the main branch."

That was the way of our town's royal family for you. Not happy unless they're making someone feel inadequate. Even one of their own. I flipped my notebook shut. "That'll do for now."

I looked over at Ivy, and she gave me a small, resigned nod.

"We'll come by your place tomorrow to check out the scene," I said. "Start working on your list of suspects. See if you can think of anyone who'd have a reason to swipe Spartacus, specifically when he was in your care."

Carl grimaced, but he nodded before standing up from the table. "I'll see you later, Uncle Marv."

Ivy and I were left in the kitchen with Marvin. He cracked a smile. "I'm glad you kids are on the case. Blasted school won't listen to a word we say. We need some proof to turn things around."

"We'll figure it out, Marv," I said. "And then we're square, right?"

"Right." He held out a hand and we shook on it. Then he offered his hand to Ivy.

"This is a megafavor, Marvin," she said, grasping it tight. "I think you're getting the better end of the deal."

"Oh, really?"

"Yup." A wicked grin flashed across her face. "But I know how to even things up."

"How's that?"

"I'm keeping the vest."

Chapter Six

The next afternoon, Ivy and I trooped across town to Carl's place. Temperatures had dropped, and a chilly wind chased us down sidewalks lined with frost-covered trees. The branches reached up into the sky like icy fingers. I looked around at the empty street and snorted. The depth of that mistake was instantly made clear. Frigid air whooshed up my nose, freezing everything in its path.

"Urgh!" I covered my nose with hands, attempting to re-direct warm air from my mouth.

"What's wrong?" Ivy zipped her coat up to her chin and inspected me.

Releasing my face, I took an experimental breath. "I'm

good," I said. "Looks like everyone else had the better sense to stay inside today."

"Sunday afternoon in Grantleyville," she said. "It's like a ghost town. So weird." Ivy moved to our town from the city over six months ago. Adjustment to small-town living was slow going. "Like, the grocery stores close at five. People still need to eat after five, Howard."

I recognized the beginnings of a rant when I saw one. "Look at it this way," I said. "Fewer people nosing around while we check out the scene of the crime, and you can come to my house after for dinner."

"It's the principle of the thing," she grouched.

"My dad's making lasagna."

"Sold."

We were closing in on Carl's house when a rhythmic thumping filled the air. Two figures darted around his drive-way as a basketball bounced between them.

Ivy rubbed her hands together and stomped her feet. "Who plays basketball outside in the middle of February?"

"Apparently our client does," I said, stopping short at the end of the drive. "Along with his poor choice of company."

Ivy followed my line of sight. She let out a breath, her whole body drooping. "This can't be good."

Carl's one-on-one partner was Miles Fletcher, proud occupant of the top slot on my list of enemies. It was a title earned when he threw away the one of my best friend. He'd joined the basketball team and spent a good chunk of last year making my life miserable. Memories of Miles's taunting voice crowded in, his laughter echoing in my mind. A flash of being shoved inside a locker, hard walls digging in to my sides. Not being able to move. The feeling of not enough air.

"Howard." Ivy snapped her fingers in front of my face. "You okay? You zoned out there for a minute."

"I'm fine."

Ivy looked ready to challenge that, and I held up a hand. "I'm fine," I said more firmly than I felt. I wasn't about to let the past interrupt my mission of closing this case as quickly as possible.

I fished a pack of Juicy out of my pocket as I strode over to Carl. He and Miles paused in their game, panting out little clouds of air into the cold. "We're here to look at your yard," I said, popping a piece of gum and talking around chomps.

Carl nodded, rubbing a red, chapped hand over an equally reddened nose. Ivy looked him over, eyeing the ball rolling over to the snowbank at the side of the yard, taking in the icicles clinging to the backboard of the net.

"Okay, I have to ask," she burst out, "why on earth are you playing outside when it is flipping freezing?"

"Carl's not going to be off the team forever," Miles said, shrugging and shifting his long arms around against the cold. "We're keeping him sharp."

"You couldn't find somewhere nice and warm to do that?" Ivy asked, tucking her hands into her pockets.

"Coach won't let him come anywhere near the court at school," Miles said. "League teams took all the times at the senior center. Nowhere else to go."

"Sounds rough," I said, heading up the drive. Chitchat was for people handing us paychecks. "Backyard?"

Carl pointed to a path leading around the side of the house and started forward. Two sets of footsteps followed along after us—one too many. Sneaking a quick look behind me, I spotted Miles keeping pace beside Ivy.

"What do you think you're doing?" I asked.

"Is this how you deal with all your clients?" Miles jogged around me. "No 'Hi, Miles, how are you, nice weather we're having'?"

"You're not my client, I don't care, and no, it's not."

He aimed a look at Ivy. "You put up with this charmer every day?"

My partner walked along beside me, kicking chunks of snow out of her way. "He's more charming than some people think they are," she said.

Miles clutched at his heart. "Direct hit."

Ivy's lips twitched.

Enough of this. We had a case to investigate. Carl stood by the gate to the backyard, watching the three of us with his usual carefully closed-off expression. I shouldered past Miles and hustled through the entrance. "Didn't get much of a deal on your Tim replacement," I muttered to Carl.

"You're not the best one to judge," he said.

Five minutes into this case and it was already giving me a headache. Definitely no more favors. I should be getting paid for this level of aggravation.

"Okay," I said, looking around the yard. "Was this where Spartacus was when he was taken?"

Carl nodded.

"Ivy, let's take a look around. You two"—I pointed at Carl and Miles—"stay back and don't touch anything."

Miles knocked off a salute. Carl rolled his eyes.

"What are we looking for, partner?" Ivy sidled up next to me.

"The usual," I said. "How they got in, how they got out."

I took in the yard. Scraggly grass poking up between bits of dirty snow. Tiny shed in the corner. A chain-link fence running around the perimeter. "The ground's too hard for there to be any prints."

"How long was Spartacus out here?" Ivy called back at Carl.

"Five, ten minutes."

"Okay," she said. "So it had to happen pretty fast."

"Over the fence?" I walked up to it to take a closer look. Bits of metal poked up along the top rail, which stood close to five feet tall. "Awfully big jump. Risk getting caught on it, too."

Ivy peered through the fence. Carl's yard backed up to an empty lot next to a convenience store. "Nothing around to use to get over it, either," she said.

A bit of black caught my eye, and I looked down. The bottom left section of the fence had a few pieces of black plastic stuck on it. "Ivy, check this out."

She crouched down beside me. "Are those zip ties?"

"I think so," I said. "Someone cut off the ends." After using them to tie the fence back together. "Wire cutters and some elbow grease. They'd be in and out pretty quick."

"I'm surprised Spartacus didn't put up more of a fuss," Ivy said.

"He'd go anywhere with anyone if they had treats for him," Carl said. He and Miles were standing directly behind us. I scowled and straightened up.

"I told you to stay over there."

"Over here looked more interesting," Miles said, towering over me to gape at the fence. "Find any more clues?"

"No," I said. "We're done." Grabbing our business cards out of my pocket, I handed one to Carl. "Get in touch if you think of any more details. Do you have that suspect list ready for me?"

"In the house." He took a step toward the back door, and I glanced over at Miles, who continued to nose around my crime scene.

"Stop touching things," I snapped at him as he poked at the fence. He shrugged as if contaminating evidence was an acceptable Sunday afternoon activity. I needed to get out of here.

"Carl." I waved him back. "The list can wait," I said. "We've got enough to get started. You can bring it tomorrow."

Carl made a noise of assent.

"We'll talk more then."

Carl nodded.

"Or we'll just keep asking questions and you can grunt yes or no."

He reached out and grabbed the collar of my lucky coat. "Less jokes," he said. "More investigating."

"Noted." I extricated myself from his meaty grasp and turned to find Ivy deep in conversation with Miles. "Hey, partner," I called out. "Time to go."

"What?" Miles sauntered over to pluck the card out of Carl's hand. "I don't get a sticky note?"

"They're business sticky notes, and no, you don't. Nobody needs to hear from you." I jerked a nod over to the gate, and Ivy and I headed out. We were halfway down the block when the thumping picked up again.

"Well, that was informative," Ivy said.

I let out a shaky breath, trying to calm my pounding heart. Inwardly, I was cursing Marvin for getting us wrapped up in this case. If we kept running into Miles like this, I'd be cursing him outwardly soon enough.

Time to focus on the positive. I jotted down notes while we walked along and hummed in agreement with Ivy's statement: "It's one step closer to being done."

"More importantly," Ivy said. "Now we're a step closer to lasagna."

Chapter Seven

Back at home, Ivy and I got to work in the garage. We were using it as a temporary office since the shack Pops and I built in the backyard would probably cave in if we tried to winterize it. I hung up our coats and Ivy switched on the space heater. Blue creaked in appreciation from her corner.

"Hey, girl." I patted her handlebars on my way to the desk. Ivy flopped down in the ugly, comfy chair as I got settled. We'd brought the essentials over for the winter move: filing cabinet, town map, resource library. My framed pictures of Humphrey Bogart as Sam Spade and Philip Marlow had made the trip as well. Pops had set up a couple of hooks so we could hang our hats underneath them.

Ivy reached out and grabbed her charcoal-gray fedora,

plopping it on her head as she put her feet up on the arm of the chair. I followed suit, setting mine at a low angle, the brown brim resting on my ears. Nothing like a good hat to get the brain juices going.

Spinning around in my chair, I looked at the map. A pin marked Carl's house, and that was about it. "We know how they got in but have no clue where they went."

"It's still more than we knew yesterday," Ivy said.

I snagged a pack of Juicy off the desk and tossed a piece in my mouth.

"Ooh, me, me." Ivy held out her hands.

"Remember that time when you were supposed to supply your own gum?" I lobbed the pack over to her. She grinned as she popped out two pieces.

"Nope."

Ah, partners. "Okay, case file," I said. "Let's write up what we got. Maybe if we're organized, we'll have this sorted out sooner rather than later."

Ivy and I flipped open our notebooks, writing up what we had gathered over the last couple of days. She jumped up when she was done, ripping her pages out and waving her hand in the air for mine. I passed the pages over and she shoved them in the filing cabinet.

"Did you put those under *C* for Carl or *D* for Dean?"

"Mine are under *P* for Pain in the Butt Pug Case, and yours are under *M* for Miles is a Jerk."

I supposed that made as much sense as any.

"Lasagna time?" Ivy did a little jig on the spot.

"Not yet." Something had been nagging at me since we left Carl's. "What was Miles talking to you about?"

"Hm?" Ivy busied herself with settling her hat back on the hook.

"When we were finishing up on the scene, Miles had you off to the side, yacking your ear off. What was that all about?"

She fiddled with her sleeve and turned to face me. "He wants to help."

I snickered, stopping when Ivy failed to join in. "Why aren't we laughing? This could only possibly be a joke."

"He knew you wouldn't listen to him, so he was trying to talk to me," she said. "Carl's his friend, and he wanted to see if he could help with the case. He doesn't want Carl booted from the team forever."

"I wouldn't trust anything Miles has to say." I tossed my own hat onto the desk and ran a hand through my hair. "There's always an angle," I said. "Only a matter of time before you figure out what it is."

"I told him we had it covered, but . . ." Ivy trailed off.

"But what?"

"He seemed really serious about it. I kind of wanted to believe him."

"Shades of old Miles rearing its head," I said. "Trust me, it won't last." I had a year's worth of anecdotal evidence to back that up. Everything from broken promises and radio silence to hallway taunts and bathroom swirlies. My friend as I had once known him was gone. Anything indicating otherwise meant trouble. "Steer clear of him, if you can. The sooner we finish this case, the sooner we can go back to avoiding Carl and pretending Miles doesn't exist."

"You don't think he could be for real?" Ivy played with the pens on the desk. "Maybe this is his way of trying to patch things up?"

"Ivy, Miles doesn't do a single thing without it suiting his own purpose. He's not trying to patch things up. If he is—" There was a thought too bizarre to wrap my head around. I wasn't about to try. "If he is, that's too bad. The damage is done."

"You wouldn't want to give him a chance, if he was?" Ivy looked up. "Trying to reach out, I mean?"

I shook my head. On my list of priorities, focusing on

reality was definitely higher than waiting for Miles to come around. "He can help Carl if he wants, but he's on his own. And he'd better stay out of our way."

"So, you're firmly Team No Forgiveness then. Shut the door and move on?" It was faint, but I caught the tiniest tremor in her voice.

"Are we still talking about Miles?"

"Mostly." Ivy sighed. "Kind of not," she said. "There was no phone call this week."

"Ah." Now I understood. Ivy's mom left her and her dad last year. That was one of the main reasons they moved to Grantleyville. Ivy had been getting into trouble, and her dad thought they needed more support, so they came to stay with her grandma. Ivy heard from her mom off and on, but things were rocky at best. "I'm sorry."

"It's fine. Whatever. My dad wanted me to call her, but I said no." Ivy scrunched her eyebrows together. "If she wants to call, she'll call. I'm not putting anything out there."

With some people, the lone guarantee was that they were going to disappoint you. "Know what I think?"

My partner looked up from the stain on the concrete floor she was attacking with the toe of her boot. "What do you think?"

"We have positively, absolutely, one-hundred-percent earned ourselves some lasagna."

Ivy rubbed her belly and let out a growly laugh. "I agree."

Grabbing our coats, I flipped off the heater, and we ran inside the house. Pops looked up from the stove as we stomped our boots on the rug. A delicious cheesy tomato smell filled the air.

"Excellent timing, kids," he said. "Supper's almost ready."

Ma came into the kitchen, a smile lighting up her face when she caught sight of Ivy. "Hi, sweetie! Are you staying for dinner?"

"If that's okay." Ivy paused in taking off her coat.

"Of course," Pops said. "You're always welcome here."

My partner grinned as Ma took her arm, towing her over to the kitchen table. "You've both been running around all weekend. We want to hear what you've been up to."

"Not so fast," my old man said as he pulled on his oven mitts. "Skip any of the bits that'll make us accessories."

"Why bother asking then?" Eileen sauntered into the kitchen and pulled up a chair.

"We can tell you a bit," Ivy said, settling in at the table. "It all started when I was at the bakery. Let me back up for a second. Has Howard told you his ridiculous policy on tackling?"

I made a mental note not to let Ivy be in charge of any future case recaps.

Chapter Eight

The next morning slunk in, dragging a drizzly, snowy rain along with it. Typical Monday dramatics. "It's not like anybody asked you to come," I muttered out the bedroom window. "You just show up." Digging through the clothes on my chair, I found a relatively clean shirt and grabbed last night's half-eaten apple off my bookshelf. Doors slammed as everyone rushed around getting ready for work and school. I wandered down to the kitchen.

"Can I get a ri—" No point in talking to an empty room. I peeked out the kitchen door in time to see my folks drive away. Rotten timing all around. My lunch and an umbrella sat on the counter. Message received. Slipping into my lucky coat, I rolled up the bottom and tied it around my waist. It'd only taken one outing to learn that in this kind of weather, floor-length, absorbent outerwear was not my friend. I threw a jacket on over it, grabbed my stuff, and ran out the door.

Ivy was waiting for me at the corner. "You look cozy."

Any retort I had fell from my lips as I gave her umbrella a once-over. "Is that a flamingo?"

"Mm, yes, it is." She twirled the pink monstrosity by its beaky handle. "Thank you for noticing."

"I think people in the next county noticed."

"I'm not explaining fashion to you again, Howard," Ivy said, turning to start the climb up Maple Street.

"Well, thank goodness for that."

We tilted our umbrellas against the elements and forged ahead. A frigid gust of wind whipped through the street, knocking us together and tangling our spokes. I sorted my umbrella out from Ivy's and looked up to see a dark figure standing in the middle of the sidewalk.

"Augh!"

"What?" Ivy whipped around. "Augh!"

Carl, dripping wet and unamused, held out a soggy piece of paper. "Suspects."

"Thanks." I grabbed the list. "Could've done without the heart attack, though. I thought it was the off-season for lurking." Tim and Carl staked this corner out all fall, relieving us of lunch items and spare change—usually by force. Winter had driven their enterprise indoors. Now they accosted kids in the school's hallways and bathrooms. Although since they'd parted ways, who knew if Tim would continue on without a heavy at his side?

Scanning through the slightly blurred names quickly, I passed the page over to Ivy. "Pretty broad pool here. Your coach. Rest of the team. Miles know he's on the list?"

"He suggested it," Carl said, holding me in a steady gaze. "Said you'd probably put him on there, anyway."

I couldn't deny it and I wasn't about to argue. Typical of Miles to take away the pleasure I'd get from writing his name down myself. "We do need to eliminate everyone," I said.

"Stoverton Stallions." Ivy looked up from the paper. "Who are they?"

"Team from the next town," Carl said. "They're our biggest rivals. Wouldn't pass up an opportunity to mess with us."

"Okay," I said. "This is a start. We'll let you know what we find out."

We took a step forward, but Carl stayed rooted in place, his wide frame blocking any exit. I glanced at Ivy and she shrugged. "Was there something else?" I asked him.

Carl shuffled his feet, rain rolling down his nose as he checked around for witnesses. Nervousness tickled the back of my neck. I didn't know whether to hear what he was leading up to or to make a break for it.

"Keep it discreet, okay?" He pulled on his ear, pained by the length of our conversation. "I don't need this all over school."

That irked me. Sure, clients did the hiring, but that didn't mean they got to dictate how to run the job. Especially when they weren't paying me. Any indication I would put in less-than-stellar work was unacceptable.

"Look, Carl," I said. "You guys came to us. We're going to run this case how we see fit. Trust us to do our job."

"Just try and stay subtle," he said, edging past us to walk down the sidewalk.

"I promise you'll get what you paid for."

Carl froze and glared back at me. "You'd think a discounted rate would mean you'd talk less."

"You know what they say: talk is cheap." I grinned and Ivy groaned.

"Quit while you're ahead," she muttered.

"We'll let you know when we have updates," I said, waving Carl away.

He stalked off toward school and we followed at an amiable pace. Ivy scratched her nose, shooting me a look. "You know, he has a small point."

"How so?"

"We're going to have to be superstealthy with this case. Have you forgotten that we're banned from investigating on school grounds? Or during the week, for that matter?"

I opened up the side door to the school and frowned as we entered the hallway. Right. That was going to make things interesting. The first case we'd worked together had gotten a little out of hand, and the school administration had overreacted. To me, it was Detection 101—if you want to solve a case, you're going to have to do a little breaking and entering. Our principal, Mrs. Rodriguez, disagreed, and parents had gotten involved. Strictly speaking, the hours of operation for Wallace and Mason Investigations were Saturday, Sunday, and every other Friday. But special cases called for special circumstances. I considered this to be emergency overtime.

"We're P.I.s," I said, heading into our classroom. "If we can't get away with a secret investigation, we should turn in our detective cards now."

Ivy and I had barely made it into our seats when the loudspeaker crackled to life. As soon as morning announcements were done, there was a knock at the door. Ms. Kowalski, our homeroom teacher, scowled as she answered it: "May I *help* you?"

Mr. Williams stepped into our classroom. "Hey, Ms. K," he said, scanning the room. "I'm looking for two of yours. Howard Wallace and Ivy Mason?"

"What business do you have with my students, Mr. Williams?" Ms. Kowalski spat out the name like it burned her tongue. There was only one reason Carl's coach would be asking to see us. I risked a peek back at Ivy. She was studiously pretending to read a book while attempting to listen in on the conversation.

"I have something urgent that I need to speak with them about," Mr. Williams continued. "They'll be back soon. Don't fret."

"We're in class, Mr. Williams. Surely this can wait." Ms. Kowalski moved to close the door.

"Afraid I have to insist," he said. "Got permission from Mrs. Rodriguez. Won't take a minute. Honest."

Ms. Kowalski sniffed and snapped her gaze back at the class. "Howard Wallace and Ivy Mason. Mr. Williams would like to see you."

Unbelievable. That had to be some kind of record-breaker for getting busted.

"So," my partner leaned across the aisle, "where do we turn our cards in?"

-. .. -.-. -.- .- -. -.. -. --- .-. .-

Ivy and I followed Mr. Williams to his office, our steps echoing in the silent hallway. He strode ahead like a man on a mission, forcing us into a near run to catch up.

Mr. Williams had a tiny space tucked away beside the locker rooms. It once was used for equipment storage, but the balls and bats had been moved to the new and improved equipment shed. The coach was not so lucky.

He fought with the wire caging that served as his door before wrenching it open and waving us in. After a quick look around, I had to give the man his due. He'd done what he could with the little he had.

Motivational posters lined the walls as well as a small shelf filled with trophies. A few framed newspaper clippings dotted the wall behind his desk—mementos of his brief college basketball career. The bit of greenery on his desk did nothing to compensate for the lingering scent of old sweat and aging rubber.

Ivy wrinkled her nose as we took our seats across from

the coach. I snuck a piece of Juicy Smash from my pocket. Maybe my taste buds could distract my nose for the duration of our visit.

"Wallace, Mason," Mr. Williams began, "thank you for coming. I have something very important I need to talk to you about."

We sat tight. Rule number eight of private investigation was never tip your hand. Better to find out what he knew before spilling our guts on the whole operation.

"This is going to come as a shock, so prepare yourselves." He took an ill-advised deep breath. "Spartacus has been kidnapped."

I blinked. "Spartacus? Who's Spartacus?" The ability to play dumb was one of the P.I.'s greatest weapons.

"Someone named their kid Spartacus?" Ivy cocked her head, playing with her hair.

Mr. Williams's jaw dropped. "He's not a kid. He's a pug."

"Oh," said Ivy. "Someone took your dog?"

"Not just my dog," Mr. Williams sputtered. "The team's dog. Our school's dog. Bred from a long line of Grantley family dogs and part of this town's rich history."

"Glad we narrowed that down," I said.

"I don't think you're taking this seriously enough." The coach leaned forward in his chair, hovering his hand over the desk. "You're here, and I need you to be up here." He held his hand up near his head.

"With all due respect, sir," I said, "we're sorry to hear about Spartacus, but what does that have to do with us?"

"I want you to find him," he said. "I know you kids solved the student council thing back in October. I think you can handle this job."

Obviously, word of our previous engagement with this case hadn't spread yet. At least he hadn't called us down to ream us out for investigating on school property. That solved the first of our problems.

"We did solve that case, Mr. Williams—"

"Call me Coach."

"We solved it, Mr. Williams," I said. "But we're also banned from investigating at school. I don't see how we can help you."

"Don't worry about that," he said. "I've already cleared things with Mrs. Rodriguez. But you have to keep it quiet. Try not to let any of the other students or teachers see you investigating. We don't want a scene."

"You want us to investigate without looking like we're investigating," Ivy said slowly. "And Mrs. Rodriguez said this was okay?" I couldn't wrap my head around it either.

Mr. Williams nodded. "You have the full support of the faculty. They want this wrapped up quick. Before Saturday."

Ivy and I exchanged an uneasy glance. This case was getting weirder by the minute. "And what's Saturday?" I asked, tugging my notebook out of my pocket.

"Do you guys even go to this school?" Mr. Williams waved away that comment, shaking his head. "I'm sorry, I'm sorry. That was offside. This whole situation has me very emotional."

"Understandable," I said.

"This Saturday is our most important game of the year. It's the annual Grudge Game between us and Stoverton." He spat into the potted plant in the corner.

"Uh, okay," Ivy said, taken aback. "And Stoverton—"

The coach spat again.

"Gross," she said under her breath. "I'm guessing this is a pretty intense rivalry?"

"One that goes back more than fifty years," he said. "We haven't lost a match in twenty. But we've been having a rough go of it this season. The guys need Spartacus if we're going to win. A mascot brings a team together. Not having one is bad luck, and bad luck has no place on a basketball court."

"Do you have any suspects?" I asked.

"One for sure," Mr. Williams said. "And unfortunately, he's one of our own, which is a darn shame."

I knew where this story led. "Who is it?"

"Carl Dean," Mr. Williams said. "Looks like a bad case of sour grapes."

"Because you benched him in favor of newer players?" Ivy piped up.

"Grantley players," I added.

"You don't know about the Grudge Game, but you've heard about that?" He rolled his eyes. "Rumors at this school get out of control. I'm trying to build the best possible team. It's about recognizing skills, not favoritism."

I wasn't sure what to make of the fact that he said that with a straight face. "But you don't think Carl sees it that way?"

"No, I do not," he said. "And I don't think he's working alone. Someone's helping him hide Spartacus. When I went by Carl's house to check things out for myself, there was no sign of Spartacus anywhere."

"You think it's another player?"

"Maybe." The coach sat back and scratched at the thinning hair beneath his cap. "Or someone in his family. Everyone knows the Deans are no good. That, or he made a deal with the devil and is working with someone from Stoverton. All I know is Spartacus is missing and someone's helping Carl cover the trail." He punctuated that sentence with another spit shot at the overwatered plant in the corner.

"I have to say that evidence of a crime is not evidence of guilt. Carl could be innocent," I said.

Mr. Williams rolled his eyes. "Then find me some proof while you're looking for Spartacus. That'll keep things tidy."

I snuck a look at Ivy, and she gave a tiny nod. Taking on the case from another angle could give us the inside track to solving it. Not that I relished the idea of "Coach" as a client.

"We'll do what we can to help you, Mr. Williams—"

"Coach."

Ivy took over before I smacked my head onto the desk. "But you're going to have to let us have access to the team."

"I don't want to get them all riled up about Spartacus," he said.

"We'll tell them we're doing a story for the school blog," I said, drawing on one of our old covers. "That way we can question them without raising any red flags."

Mr. Williams nodded slowly, steepling his fingers under his broad chin. "Okay," he said. "That could work."

We rose from our seats. "About our fees," I said.

"I can't pay you, Wallace," he said. "We've got to keep this strictly under the table."

I started to protest, and he waved a hand at me. "Let's make a deal. Find Spartacus, and aside from the immeasurable school pride you will earn, I'll also give you both extra credit for track and field."

Cold, hard cash was always preferable, but a free pass on running around in the hot sun was nothing to sneeze at. Contemplating that, I swung a look at Ivy, who shrugged. "Enough credit to skip long jump?"

"Sure," Mr. Williams said, rattling open the cage door for us to leave. It came to mind that a contract wouldn't be out of order for this one. I wouldn't put it past the coach to try to wriggle out of his end of the bargain. Ivy and I headed toward class, steeling ourselves for Ms. Kowalski's evil eye.

"Guess we better get cracking on finding this dog," my partner said. "The clients are starting to pile up."

"And yet, no one is paying us."

Chapter Nine

"This wasn't what I had in mind for our lunch meeting, Ivy," I said, plopping down into the chair beside her.

"It's called multitasking, Howard." She rearranged the wrapped cookies on the table in front of us. "We're helping with the bake sale *and* working the case. Easy peasy."

"But why?"

"Because the Arts Council needs money. They are buh-roke."

"Still not explaining why we're here."

"Sale's running all week. All the groups have to help out, including Drama Club. Remember that time you made me join Drama Club?"

"That was a cover. For a case. You don't have to keep going."

Ivy shrugged. "I like it."

"I'll try to make the best of it, I guess." I reached out to pick up a large chocolate chip cookie when a quiet voice piped up.

"You have to pay for that."

"What?"

A girl peeked around from the other side of Ivy, blinking behind thick, green-framed glasses. "The cookie," she said. "You have to pay for it." She blinked again. "Um, please?"

I looked back and forth between her and Ivy. "Who? Why? Ivy?"

Sighing, Ivy leaned back in her chair. "Howard, this is Ashi Jenkins. She's in band, and unlike you, was actually scheduled to work this shift of the bake sale with me. Do you mind if he hangs out, Ashi?"

Ashi smiled and ducked her head. "Not as long as he pays for the cookie. Ellis said no freebies. We need the money."

"Who's Ellis?"

"Ellis Garcia," Ashi said. "She's the head of the Student Arts Council. This was all her idea."

"You know bake sales are an inefficient way to raise

money," I said, gesturing at the rest of the table with the cookie in my hand. "It's an unreliable, unsustainable source of income."

"You have a better idea?" Ivy quirked an eyebrow at me. "Think we should start an Arts Council detective agency?"

"Oooh," Ashi said. "I have the perfect coat."

Ivy snorted out a laugh and I grinned. "I like you, Ashi. You're alright." Pulling back the plastic on the cookie, I took a bite.

"That's four dollars," Ashi said.

I paused midchew, opening my mouth to let the chunk of cookie fall back onto the table.

"Ew, Howard." Ivy wrinkled her nose at me.

"I take it all back. You'll make a killing with prices like that."

The girls stared at me until I sighed and pulled a crumpled bill out of my pocket. "Keep the change," I said, wiping my mangled cookie off the table. "Consider it my contribution to the cause."

Ivy plucked the money out of my hand with a smirk. "I'll consider it a start."

A crowd of kids came up to the table. Ashi and Ivy were soon busy handing out treats and collecting funds. I leaned back in my chair, rummaging through my bag for my lunch. The situation was less than ideal. Ivy and I needed to talk about the case. Hard to do while she was hawking brownies and butter tarts. Ever harder with Ashi around—there was such a thing called client confidentiality.

I ate my lunch in the loudest amount of silence I could manage. Ivy glanced over as I crunched on a carrot and burst out laughing. "Pouty McPoutface, relax," she said. "We'll get to the case."

"During this lunch period, or are you penciling me in for sometime this week?"

"Gimme a sec." Ivy waved a hand at me as she got swept up in another wave of kids. I felt Ashi's eyes on me. She pushed her glasses up the bridge of her nose with one finger and squinted.

"You took another cookie." It wasn't a question.

It also wasn't wrong.

I pulled the ginger cookie out of my sleeve and stuffed it in my mouth before handing over another bill. Ashi gave it a quick inspection and popped it in their cash box. If Ivy and I ever managed to expand the business, we were stealing Ashi away from the band.

Things finally slowed down at the table. Ivy thunked

a hand against her forehead. "I gave that kid the wrong change. Ashi, can you give this back to him?"

"Who?" Ashi craned her neck, following Ivy's finger.

"Over in the far corner. In the red shirt on the other side of the cafeteria."

"Oh, sure." Ashi hopped up, dollar in hand, scooting away from the table.

Ivy turned to me. "Okay, we gotta talk fast. It won't take her long to get back."

"What?" My sugar-laden brain tried to connect Ivy's dots.

"Howard. Case, focus, talk."

"Right, okay. So we have two clients and one case."

"And about a million suspects," Ivy said, pulling Carl's wrinkled list out of her pocket.

"Give or take," I agreed. "We should focus on the ones closest to home first. Rule out the obvious."

My partner nodded as she pursed her lips, scanning the list. "Good thing we're starting with the team then. Speaking of the team . . ." Ivy trailed off.

I knew exactly where this was going. "I'll be fine," I said, somewhat snappier than I had intended.

"All I was going to say was maybe I should handle questioning Miles. It might make things a little easier."

"I don't need you to baby me, Ivy."

"It's not babying. I'm just trying to help. I know things are—"

"I can deal with Miles Fletcher," I said.

"Miles?" Ashi bounced up to the table. "From the basketball team? He's cute."

"Ashi," I said. "I thought we were friends."

"Only if you pay for the brownie you snuck."

Chapter Ten

After school, Ivy and I stood outside of the gym, listening to the pounding of feet vibrating through the doors. Starting with the team made sense. They were the ones who'd had the most access to Spartacus. A good detective eliminated all of the possibilities.

"We going in?" Ivy placed a hand on the door. "Or should we gawk at the door some more?"

A *good* detective could stomach questioning a roomful of jerks who once stole all his clothes during gym and then shoved him into the girls' locker room.

A *great* detective would do it without hesitation.

I'd file that under Goals. Taking a deep breath, I pushed on the other door. "We're going in." Once inside, we were met with a wall of sound: thumping basketballs, squeaking shoes, shouts, and high-fives.

"So, this is how the sportsball half lives," Ivy said, scanning the room. "Looks sweaty."

"Let's make this quick." We walked the length of the gym, keeping close to the bleachers, out of the danger zone. Grantleyville didn't skimp when it came to their sporting venues, so the space was large for a middle school. High windows let in enough natural light to showcase the green-and-gold gladiator painted on the floor. A small stage at one end housed the audiovisual room and spare mats behind the curtains.

"Why are there people here?" Ivy nodded at the seated kids scattered around the bleachers. Most were clustered together, but one girl sat at the far end, face hidden by bright blue bangs as she tapped away at her phone.

"Friends? Fans? I don't know," I said as we reached the end of the gym. "One mystery at a time."

Mr. Williams spotted us and blew his whistle in two short bursts. "Come on in, guys," he said. "We need to talk."

The team jogged over and set up in a semicircle around us and their coach. Eyeing me and Ivy with varying degrees of curiosity and hostility, the players began to mutter among themselves.

"Settle down, settle down," Mr. Williams said. "Howard and Ivy are here today at my request. They're doing a story on the team."

The rumbling increased. I noticed the blue-haired girl taking an interest.

One of the players raised his hand. "Aren't those the detective kids?" So much for going incognito.

"No, no," Mr. Williams chuckled nervously. "You're thinking of someone else. Now be quiet and let me talk. Howard and Ivy are reporting on the Grudge Game for the school blog, getting everyone excited about the big day."

"Coach, come on." Another player stepped forward, and I bit back a groan. Vince Neely—five foot six inches of insolent aggression, usually directed at me. Miles had surrounded himself with some quality new friends. "We're not idiots," Vince said, keeping his voice low. "This is about Spartacus, right?" He rolled his eyes in our direction. "You're really going to let him handle it?"

The coach sputtered while the rest of the team started nodding and whispering furiously over one another.

"Did Carl really take Spartacus?"

"What are they going to do?"

Obviously someone had to be the voice of reason here. I

took a deep breath, ready to shout down the chorus of questions, when someone beat me to it. One loud voice pealed out above the rest: "Why don't you have professionals handle it?" I locked eyes with the speaker and fought the urge to roll my eyes. Of course. Miles. So much for wanting to help with the case.

"I mean," Miles said, quieter now that he had the group's attention, "we want Spartacus *found*, right? Why mess around?"

Vince high-fived him, and Mr. Williams blew a quick chirp on his whistle.

"That's enough, Fletcher," he said. "Everyone, bring it in close." The circle cinched tight as Mr. Williams huddled the players up. "Are you telling me all of you know about Spartacus?" He looked around the nodding faces. "Honestly, I can't keep anything from you kids," Mr. Williams muttered. "I wanted to do this quietly. Okay. Listen up. Team info only. Howard and Ivy are doing us a favor. I expect everyone to cooperate and keep it to themselves. Answer their questions fully and with respect. Back to shooting drills in the meantime."

Miles shot me a look as Vince tugged him over to the rest of their gang. Deep breaths, Howard. One step at a time. Best way to handle this was to be professional. And fast.

"Divide and conquer?" I asked Ivy. She glanced around at the players, who had separated themselves into two groups, one at each basket on either end of the gym.

"The sooner we're out of here, the better," she said and then pointed at the youngest, scrawniest looking player on the left side. "I'm gonna start with the little one." Ivy strode down the length of the bleachers, culling her chosen player from the crowd and leading him over to a quiet corner. Poor little guy.

Little being a relative term. All of the players had at least a solid few inches on me. I squared my shoulders, not about to let myself be intimidated.

Nothing wrong with starting with a friendly face. Wandering over to my end of the gym, I zeroed in on the single one in the crowd of meatheads. "Scotty."

The tall blond sixth-grader spun around, twitching a basketball nervously between his hands. "What's up, Howard? Crazy about Spartacus, eh? Are you figuring out who took him? Do you think it was really Carl? Do you think it was me?"

Scotty Harris, former client, occasional informant, terrible musician.

"How're things, Scotty?"

"Everyone's freaked out about Spartacus being gone, especially with the big game on Saturday." A frown marred his round friendly face. "I still can't believe it."

"Were you on the care roster?"

"Yeah, even though my whole family's allergic. Coach said no one was allowed to skip," he said. "Even the guys who aren't playing much. They thought that was a load."

"Right, because of the new kids." I nodded out to the rest of the team taking shots at the net. "Point out the newbies to me."

"Uh, those five down there." Scotty pointed out a quintet of obvious Grantleys. Even their shoes looked put out with having to walk among the common folk. "And that guy over there."

"The one using his head to bounce the ball?"

Scotty sighed. "Yup."

Mr. Williams had made some top-notch additions to the team.

"Guys, guys!" One of the older players jogged up to the new kids, concern creasing his forehead. "We're practicing shooting at the net, not each other."

"Who's that?"

"Oscar, our captain," Scotty said. "Well, for now, anyway. Coach is talking about picking a new one if we don't start playing better. Like that's Oscar's fault." He looked over at the newbs. "Probably just an excuse to pick a Grantley."

"Heard much chatter from the team?"

"Lots," he said. "People are freaked out about Spartacus. Worried about the game. Mad at Carl."

"They think he did it?"

Scotty shrugged. "Some of them."

"You?"

"Carl's a good guy."

I halted my pen at that comment and raised an eyebrow at Scotty.

"To me," he amended. "And when he's not hanging out with Tim."

"Heard that's not an issue anymore. So, who would you peg?"

"Aw, Howard." Scotty hugged the basketball to his stomach, drooping at the request.

"If you had to take a guess."

He bounced the ball a few times while he pondered the question. "I heard Oscar might be transferring to Stoverton by the end of the month," he said. We both looked over at the captain, who was pulling on his hair as two players collided mid–jump shot. "His parents want him to have more play time. End the year on a winning team before going to high school."

Interesting. "Thanks, Scotty."

I turned to find another player to talk to and almost got taken out by the basketball flying at my head. I slapped it away, relieved my survival instincts had passed another test. The ball bounced harmlessly on the ground as my assailant came into view.

"You're supposed to catch it," Miles said. "I guess I'm up next."

"Don't tell me how to run my investigation," I said, kicking the ball back at him. Miles stopped it with his foot, picking it up to spin it neatly in the air. "I can't even cooperate without getting my head bitten off."

"This is cooperating?" I scoffed.

"I'll make it easy for you," he said. "I had nothing to do with it, I don't know who did. End of story."

The rhythmic pounding of the basketballs in the gym mixed with my rising aggravation at Miles. I felt the words snapping out before I registered them. "Enjoying your bench time lately? Having a nice, relaxing season?"

"It's great, the new guys are fine," Miles shot the ball back to me with a hard bounce. "Don't mind it at all."

I narrowly avoided catching the ball with my chin. "No reason to be mad at Coach?" Bouncing the ball a few times to get the weight of it, I slammed it back to Miles with a final dig. "Take a little payback?"

He barely flinched as he caught the ball and returned fire. I caught a glimpse of Ivy watching us from the other end of the gym. A voice in my head yelled at me to stop, but it was drowned out by memories of Miles—stuffing me in a locker, throwing my lunch on the ground, telling me we were never friends. I whipped the basketball back as hard as I could. "You're not above a nasty trick?"

"I don't mess with innocent animals," Miles said, squeezing the ball between his hands. "Only jerks."

"Howard!" Ivy called out. I turned to see her speed-walking over to us with a look of concern on her face. A scathing reply for Miles was on the tip of my tongue when I looked back to see the ball flying toward my face. All my instincts deserted me, leaving my cheek and nose to step up to the plate. They managed to catch the sucker in one go.

Pain, bright and furious, clouded my vision. I fell backward onto the floor, the thump of my landing broken by a gasp from Ivy and Miles calling for Mr. Williams. A light flashed, and there was the telltale click as someone snapped a picture.

Like I'd need help remembering this moment.

Chapter Eleven

"What do you think?" I lifted the ice pack from my face, leaning back in Mr. Williams's desk chair. "I think it makes me look tough. Don't you think it makes me look tough?"

Ivy examined the darkening bruise on my cheek. "I think it makes you look like you caught a basketball with your face."

"Thanks," I grimaced—and then fought the urge to grimace over the grimace. Almost any facial expression brought a new level of pain.

"On the bright side," Ivy said, "it stopped bleeding. And no broken nose, no concussion."

Mr. Williams had checked me out, pronouncing me mostly fine, if not coordinated, but insisted I take some time icing my wounds. He'd called my folks, who wanted to come pick me up, but I needed some fresh air and time to debrief with Ivy. The team was long gone, putting a pin in our interrogations for now. I tossed the ice pack back on the coach's desk. "Let's get out of here." We walked out into the hallway.

"Howard."

Apparently not all of the team had gone home. Miles straightened up from his post holding up the wall. "You okay?"

"What are you doing here?" I staggered closer to him. "Waiting for round two of Hit Howard with Blunt Objects?"

"It was an accident."

"As far as games go, I give it zero stars. Ten out of ten would not play again—wait, what?" My battered brain sluggishly computed the quiet words Miles had uttered.

"It was an accident," he said again, slowly and deliberately. "I thought you'd catch it. Not my fault you have zero coordination."

The fluorescent lights buzzed overhead as Miles and I stared at each other in silence.

"Right. Of course. It was completely my fault." I chuckled, and Miles shifted uncomfortably. My face was screaming at me, but I couldn't stop the streams of laughter bursting out of my mouth.

"Howard," Ivy murmured, tugging at my arm.

"Why are you here?" I asked Miles as I shrugged off her hand.

"I wanted to make sure you were okay," he said, rubbing at the back of his neck. "I was worried."

"Over a year," I said, walking up to Miles until he backed into a wall. "Over a year of you making fun of me, shoving me, ignoring me. Now you're concerned?"

"You were bleeding," Miles said. "I almost knocked you out."

"Trust me, you've done worse."

Miles studied the floor. "I don't know what to say," he muttered. "I just—"

"Need to go," I said. "Please go away." I rubbed at my temple where a headache was beating at a furious tempo.

"I wanted to talk about the case," Miles said, shocking my eyes back open.

"The professionals are handling it." Ivy stepped between us. "He asked you to go away, and he asked nicely," she said. "I wouldn't bet on me doing the same."

Miles's jaw twitched as he set his teeth. He opened his mouth, clicked it shut, then gave his head a small shake and walked away.

Ivy tugged on my arm. “Howard, come on. Let’s get you home.”

“ ‘*The professionals are handling it.*’ ” I snorted. “That was good.” Ivy smiled as I bumped my shoulder against hers. “I could have taken him,” I said.

“For sure.” She nodded.

“But for the record, basketballs aren’t my usual weapon of choice.”

“I’m afraid to ask what is.”

“Deductive reasoning, quick wit, running away.” I counted off on my fingers and lost track. “I have a wide variety of skills.”

“I know,” she said, patting my back as we left the school. Puddles still dotted the sidewalk down Maple Street. I weaved around them, feeling a bit sick. Walking might not have been the best plan.

“You sure you’re okay?” Ivy asked.

“Yeah,” I said. “Kind of a headache, that’s about it.”

“Good,” she said, planting herself in front of me, taking a deep breath. “Then we can talk about how you lost your flipping mind in there. What were you thinking?”

“Be nice to me, I’m wounded.”

“You’re fine.” She brushed off my moaning. “But that bizarro stand-off with Miles? Not cool.”

I didn't expect her to understand. My history with Miles was dark and tangled long before Ivy came along.

"Our case involves the team," she said. "He is on the team. We're going to run into him a lot, so you're going to have to learn to deal with it."

The most annoying part of having a partner was when she was right. "It won't happen again," I muttered.

"Nobody's perfect, Howard Wallace. I'd have been tempted to get in a basketball-flinging match with him, too." Ivy slung an arm over my shoulder. "Did you find out anything useful before the testosterone started flying?"

I filled her in on Scotty's tip concerning Oscar's possible move.

"Interesting," she said. "The little dude I was talking to said Oscar's best friend is the captain of the Stoverton team."

"We need to check out Oscar," I said.

"Agreed." Ivy and I spun around at the unfamiliar voice. The blue-haired girl from the gym was standing behind us. Now that we were face to face, recognition clicked in.

I recognized we were in trouble.

"Howard?" Ivy looked back and forth between me and the newcomer, picking up on the tense vibe. Seemed it was up to me to make the proper introductions.

"Ivy, this is Leyla Bashir, the editor of the *Grantleyville Middle School Blog*," I said. Holding out a hand to Leyla, I aimed for a charming grin. "We've never met, but I've enjoyed your work."

"Funny you should bring that up," she said.

"Funny, ha-ha, or funny, uh-oh?" Ivy asked.

"You tell me." Leyla's smile went sharp and flinty, ready to strike. "How is it that you enjoy my work, we've never met, but apparently you're also reporters for the blog?"

The problem with a good cover story is that if you use it too many times, eventually you get burned. "There's been a misunderstanding," I said. "The other day, Ivy and I were talking about how great the blog is and how we'd like to work on it. Someone told you different, they got the wrong end of the stick."

"That is odd," Leyla said, tapping her chin. "I heard Mr. Williams say you were working on a story about the basketball team. Which is why *I* was there. Does he know something I don't?"

"Weird," Ivy said. "I think this Grudge Game has him pretty stressed out."

"Now we're getting to it." Leyla crossed her arms. "I'm a reporter, Wallace. I know stall tactics when I hear them," she said. "More importantly, I know a story. Let's cut to the chase. Tell me what you've got on the missing mascot case."

Word about Spartacus was bound to get around, but I'd been hoping it wouldn't travel quite so fast. "Missing mascot?" Best not to contribute to the gossip mill. "First we're hearing about it," I said.

"You expect me to believe you were heading into basketball practice for kicks?" Leyla shook her head. "Bit of a stretch, given your history with a good portion of the team."

She dug through her bag and pulled out her phone. "Let me refresh your memory," she said, scrolling through her notes. "Spartacus the pug was stolen from the yard of one Carl Dean last Tuesday evening. Carl has since been suspended from the team, and Coach Williams hired the two of you to track down his beloved mascot. How am I doing so far?"

"How'd you find all that out?" Ivy craned her neck to sneak a peek at Leyla's screen.

"I hear things." Leyla dropped her phone back in her bag and snapped it shut. "Things like Carl's maintaining his innocence, so who've you got your eye on?"

Cards-on-the-table time. "We're working the case," I said. "But we can't risk the investigation by talking about it."

"What about a little cooperation?" Leyla leaned in, a

spark in her brown eyes. "Think about it. You let me in on the details; I pass along anything I find out. I get huge headlines and make us all famous."

Getting our names out there would mean bigger cases and more money. But I couldn't jeopardize an active case. "We're gonna pass," I said. "If we put information out there before everything's locked away, we risk tipping off whoever's behind this. Finding Spartacus is the priority."

Leyla shrugged. "I'll hold the story until you solve it."

Ivy motioned me over to the side. "Hang on," I said to Leyla. My partner and I took a few steps back to confer.

"I don't like this," Ivy said. "It feels wrong. Like we're trading in Marvin and Spartacus for bigger jobs."

"Jobs that would pay," I said.

Ivy gave me a hard look. "Howard. What happened to worrying about our reputations?"

"Let me put it another way," Leyla said, stepping toward our huddle. "Work with me and I'll let the fake reporter thing go. Don't let me in, I rat you out for misusing the blog's name. Make it our top story. Blow your cover. You'll look completely incompetent. What do you think that'll do to your reputation?"

She had us up against the wall. If it was happening to

anyone else, I'd be impressed. Instead I was stuck with a last-resort pity card. "You'd put a story ahead of the safety of a poor little dog?"

"Either way, I'm getting a great story," Leyla said.

My partner's jaw dropped. "That's cold."

"That's the news," Leyla fired back. "We have a deal?"

"No press until the case is done," I said. "And if anyone asks about us being reporters, you'll back up the story. We'll share as much as we can in the meantime."

Leyla held out a hand. "And then I get to print the full deal."

"Agreed," I said as we shook. Leyla walked with us, and we filled her in on everything we'd learned so far, which took a frustratingly short amount of time.

"Focusing on the team first makes a lot of sense," she said. "Odds are pretty good for an inside job."

"Looks that way. Here's our card." I pulled a business card out of my pocket and stuck it to her palm. "Keep in touch."

"That's a—"

"We know," Ivy said. "Makes 'em harder to lose."

-. .. -.-. -.-   .- -. -..   -. --- .-. .-

Our business with Leyla all sorted, Ivy and I made plans to meet early in the morning and went our separate ways.

Midway up the drive, I decided to stop by the office before heading inside. I checked on Blue in her corner, adjusting her blanket and wiping the dust off her headlamp. Her handlebars swung to the side with a creak and I rolled my eyes. "Don't start," I said, shielding my cheek from her reproving glare. "It's a bruise. It'll be fine."

Sitting at my desk, I started a file on our new friend Leyla and wrote up everything we'd learned today. Not much. I rested my pounding head on my notebook. Missing dog. Disgruntled team. Possible inside job. Frankly, I still wasn't entirely convinced our client wasn't the culprit. Great start, all in all. I stuffed the notes into the filing cabinet and headed inside.

Pops was waiting for me in the kitchen. "Lemme see." He tilted my chin back to examine my cheek under the kitchen lights. "You got clocked real good," he said, shaking his head. "Put some more ice on it before dinner." I could see a hundred questions swimming in his eyes, but Pops did me a favor and rolled them all into one. "Miles?"

"It was mostly an accident." I shrugged.

"It's the not *mostly* part that concerns me," he said. "What were you doing at the practice, anyway?"

"Helping Ivy with a story for the blog," I said, grabbing an ice pack out of the freezer.

Pops paused his stirring of the chili on the stove and tossed me a tea towel. "The school blog? Ivy's writing for them now? And she needed your help?"

I wrapped the ice pack in the towel and held it over my face. "That's what friends are for," I said.

"Right." He stared at me before resuming the stirring. "Go set the table."

Eileen sauntered into the kitchen "I heard you're into sports now, Howeird," she said, trying to poke at my face. I fended her off with the ice pack. "The shiner's a mild improvement." She grabbed the pack and smacked me on the arm with it. "Makes you look tough."

Well, at least there was that.

Chapter Twelve

It was 8 a.m. and I'd been waiting at the corner for fifteen minutes before realizing my partner had stood me up. In another five I'd be concerned. Considering my phone privileges were in a constant state of revocation, I had no way to check on her. Looked like I was hoofing it solo.

As the wind pierced my coat and I dodged around poorly plowed sidewalks, I began mentally calculating how many days until spring. The number was obnoxiously high. "Blue's got the right idea," I muttered.

"Talking to yourself, Howard?"

I stuck a finger in my ear and wiggled it, squinching up my eyes. "I seem to be hearing things."

Miles fell into step beside me and snorted. "Very funny."

"Apparently it was more wishful thinking than joke." I quickened my pace and Miles's long legs easily matched my stride.

"Look," he held up his hands, "we need to talk."

"Did the basketball ricochet off my face and hit you, too? Why this sudden need to communicate?" Annoyance, indignation, and too many coats brought my temperature to the boiling point. I halted in the middle of the sidewalk to unzip my top layer and let the steam out. Miles stood beside me, cool as a cucumber.

"Go away," I said between a huff and a puff.

"Listen, I know things have been bad between us," he said, eyeing my admittedly spectacular shiner. "Hear me out. Please."

Every instinct was telling me to keep on walking. Every one except for the little voice that said, "Wait a minute." It was one little voice that apparently had a direct line to my mouth. "You have thirty seconds." Curiosity always seemed to outweigh self-preservation.

"I already talked to Ivy, but I should have come to you. I shouldn't have gone behind your back. Carl's my friend, and he's in trouble. I want to help with his case."

"Since when are you and Carl such good friends?"

"He's a good guy. We get along. We talk a lot."

"Carl . . ." I raised an eyebrow. "Talking?"

"He doesn't just like me because I'm good at basketball," Miles said, kicking at the snowbank.

"Some people liked you despite that fact," I said, zipping up my coat against the chilly air that had finally cooled me down.

"Yeah, well, he doesn't hold it against me either," Miles said.

"There are so many other things to hold against you, I can see why it wouldn't be high on his list."

Miles clenched his fists and stared at his shoes. When he looked back up, all signs of fight had cleared away. "He's my friend," he repeated. "And I want to help."

"Because you were so helpful yesterday." I started back down the sidewalk. His thirty seconds had been up for a while.

"I lost my temper." Miles loped alongside me. "You were pushing my buttons, but that's no excuse. Look, I'll hire you." He pulled some worn bills and coins out of his pocket and held them out.

"You clean the couch out for all of that?" I shoved his hand back. "Can't buy your way onto the case, Miles."

He ran a hand over his shaved scalp and growled. "Why do you have to twist everything?" Miles pulled a knitted Gladiators hat out of his pocket. Jammed it on his head. "Is it so hard to believe that I could be trying to do something good?"

For the second time that morning, I found myself wishing for Ivy to show up. I was in serious need of backup.

Miles sighed and shook his head. "I knew this would be a waste of time. I don't know what I was expecting."

"Wait," I said as he turned to walk away. Miles looked as surprised as I felt to hear that word pop out. Ivy was right. I should have gone to the doctor.

"Your captain," I said slowly.

"Oscar," Miles supplied.

"We need to talk to him, and I'd rather not go through a whole basketball team to do it. You want to help? Get us introduced."

Miles nodded with growing enthusiasm. "I can do that. I can definitely do that."

"Fine. Great," I said. "I'll see you at lunch."

He started forward and then took a step back. "See you, Howard," Miles said before taking off at a jog toward the school.

-. .. -.-. -.-   .- -. -..   -. --- .-. .-

I stood by Ivy's locker, chewing the run-in with Miles over in my brain. Letting him help felt like a mistake as soon as he'd left. I'd be an idiot to trust him. And yet, if he could ease our access to the team, why not make use of that? I checked out the clock on the wall. Five minutes until the bell. Hopefully my partner showed up soon, or I'd have no time to fill her in on this new development.

She erupted through the side door with a bang, rushing down the hall in a flurry of bags, coat, and limbs, and made a beeline for her locker. "Glad you're alive," I said as I propped up a slice of wall beside her.

"What?" She looked up from emptying her bag and the connection sparked in her eyes. "We were supposed to meet. I'm so sorry," Ivy said. She was breathless, and her hair was flying out of a messy bun. "Weird night. I slept in. Got in a fight with my dad—"

"Did he forget to drink his orange juice again?" I laughed.

"Something like that." Ivy shrugged off her coat and flung it inside the depths of her locker. "Anyway, it made me super-late, and my grandma had to drive me here. This Tuesday is such a Monday."

"Tell me about it. Miles tried to bribe his way into the case this morning."

"You're kidding."

"I wish I was. He had a fistful of cash to prove it."

"Seriously?"

"Well, maybe more like a fingerful, but same idea."

She grabbed a pack of Juicy from her pocket and popped a piece. "What'd you say?" she asked, handing the pack over.

I busied myself with snagging a couple of pieces and carefully sliding the pack neatly back in its case.

"Oh, Howard. You didn't take his money, did you?"

"What? No." Snapping a piece of gum between my teeth, I tossed the pack into the bag Ivy was still rummaging through. "Imayhavesaidhecouldhelp," I muttered.

"Say that again?" Ivy paused mid-dig.

"He kept asking to help, and he actually *can* help in certain areas, so I thought: keep your friends close and your enemies closer. At least this way, if he's involved, we can keep an eye on him."

"You aren't allowed to walk to school by yourself anymore," she said, stuffing her bag onto the small shelf.

"And whose fault was that?"

Ivy grabbed a couple of books before slamming her locker shut and turning to face me. "It's ridiculous."

"I realize it's not my best executive decision, but *ridiculous* is a little harsh. You were the one who said I needed to learn to deal with running into him. 'Consider a second chance' and all that?"

"No, not *you* ridiculous," she said. "Well, a little you, but I meant Miles. How he's treated you this past year? Has he forgotten yesterday?" We headed down the hallway together. "He comes up with a plan and you're just supposed to roll with it? Who does he think he is? How many chances does he think he gets?"

There. That was the killer backup I needed this morning.

"You can't be in someone's life whenever it's convenient for you," Ivy said, building up some steam. "Make plans and expect them to fall in line."

"Where's Miles?" I looked around. "He's missing all the good stuff now. We should write this down."

"Right," Ivy said, blinking up at me. "Miles. I'm going to be watching him like a hawk. One little sneer and he's out."

"Sounds completely reasonable to me," I said.

"What's the plan for today?" she asked, juggling the books in her hands.

"Tracking down Oscar, Mr. Team Captain," I said. "Asking pointed questions. Getting some answers."

"All good ideas," Ivy said, narrowing her eyes. "What the heck is that?"

I followed her gaze to a poster hanging up outside our classroom, advertising the Grudge Game. "I guess they have to sell tickets somehow."

She marched over to the wall and ripped the sign down.

"Or not," I said. "We could suggest the face-to-face approach to them."

"Look what they did," Ivy pointed to the wall. The Grudge Game sign had been covering up another poster. A meticulously hand-decorated one for the Arts Council bake sale. Ivy must have spotted the sparkles creeping out around the sides. "There's plenty of wall to go around," she grumbled. "This is ridiculous."

"Mr. Williams probably had one of the newbies put it up," I said. "They saw that one and thought: *This where signs go. Shiny. Put sign here.* Honest mistake."

"Ha. Ha." Ivy crumpled up the offending paper and tossed it in the recycling bucket as we entered our classroom. It hit the rim and rolled across the floor.

Ms. Kowalski looked up from her desk, eyes glinting at the opportunity to shed the morning's first blood. "Howard Wallace," she barked. "Kindly refrain from littering in my classroom." A purple-painted talon extended, its razor-sharp edge pointing at the incriminating piece of refuse. Ivy waggled her eyebrows at me and scuttled over to her seat. Lucky escape. I could argue the accusation, but when it came to Ms. Kowalski, I'd rather lose a battle to win the war.

With an admirable amount of restraint, I held back a smart reply, picked up the paper, and placed it in the bin. Once I was seated, I pulled my notebook out of my pocket and flipped to the back. As the frequency of my run-ins with my homeroom teacher increased throughout the year, I'd thought it would be best to start keeping track. Records always came in handy. I put a tick under Ms. Kowalski's name, then did a quick tally. And smiled.

I was still ahead by two.

Chapter Thirteen

From an investigative standpoint, the cafeteria had its fair share of strengths and weaknesses. The noise and general chaos provided ample coverage for a stealth chat. But when you crossed social boundary lines to have that chat, stealth went out the window.

Stares dogged our every move as we met up with Miles by the bake sale table. Ashi looked more than a little curious, and she wasn't alone.

"People are looking at us," Miles murmured.

"Feel free to leave," Ivy said.

"No." He squared his shoulders. "We're doing this. Come on." Miles led the way over to the basketball team's table, ignoring the whispers as he dodged a few pointed looks.

The team was crowded around their table, with Oscar reigning from the end. His rangy limbs were draped over his seat as he studiously ignored our approach.

Miles stepped up first and whispered a few words to him. Oscar frowned and shook his head.

"Oh, yes, he's very helpful," Ivy said to me. Miles kept talking, and I made a mental note to add lipreading to our training manual. My partner was right: this wasn't working. I moved forward just as Miles straightened up.

"For Carl," he said, and Oscar nodded. Miles waved us over. Ivy and I slid out a couple of extra chairs along the way and pulled up the seats beside the captain. Miles clapped him on the shoulder and left to go buy lunch. The rest of the players inched their chairs away from us, and Oscar scoffed. "Thanks, guys."

"Didn't get a chance to talk with you yesterday, Oscar," I said, pulling out my notes from the day before.

Oscar glanced at us and then concentrated on his sandwich. "You seemed busy," he said. "Bleeding all over our court."

"That did actually take up a lot of time," Ivy agreed.

"You're the captain," I said. "You know your guys better than anyone. Think any of them could've taken Spartacus?"

Oscar's sharp eyes cut down the line at the table. "No," he said. "No way."

"Really." I tapped my pen against my notebook. "Not even someone like, for instance, Miles?"

"What?" Oscar snapped his head up and scowled.

"Wanted to make sure you were listening," I said.

Ivy leaned in, whisper-singing in my ear, "Focus."

"Okay, fine," I said, waving her away. "None of your teammates. Let's look at the next logical option: the Stoverton Stallions."

"The Stallions?" Oscar looked warily at us, and Ivy bounced in her seat.

"You didn't do the thing," she said.

"What thing?"

"The spitting thing everyone does," Ivy said, pointing at the team who were, in fact, midspit. She set her elbows on the table and squinted at Oscar. "Got some warm fuzzies for Stoverton, buddy?"

"I think it's dumb to hate a whole town, if that's what you mean," Oscar said, hunched over in his chair. "I have friends who live in Stoverton."

Now we were getting to it. "Yes," I said. "Captain of the Stoverton Stallions–type friends."

Oscar sighed. "Jake and I've been friends for a lot longer than we've been on opposite teams. What's your point?"

"Heard you're thinking about making a switch," Ivy said. She was met with silence.

"If you're going to play for a new team," I said, "might as well be the one with the bragging rights. Isn't Stoverton having a pretty good season this year?"

"I wouldn't do that to the guys." Oscar set his jaw and doubled down on his sandwich.

We were losing him. Time to barrel through the rest of the questions before we were forcibly relocated back to our natural habitat in the undesirable sector of the cafeteria.

"You know Stoverton—you hang with their team," I said. "Any of them recently acquire a dog?"

"You think I wouldn't recognize if one of them started walking around with Spartacus?" Oscar paused mid-drink, nostrils flaring. "These are the kinds of questions you ask? How do you solve any cases?"

"What about Captain Jake? He planning anything extra special for the Grudge Game?"

"He's not like that," Oscar said, shaking his head. "I've known Jake since we were five. He's like my brother."

"A long history isn't exactly a solid alibi," Ivy said.

"We were hanging out on Tuesday," Oscar said. "There's no way it was him."

"Maybe he was distracting you," I said. "Did he say anything strange or—"

An odd look crossed Oscar's face.

"What? What did you think of?"

"Nothing," he said.

"If you thought of it," Ivy said. "It's not nothing."

Oscar leaned down, lowering his voice. "Jake was talking about a kid on his team," he said. "He's into pranks, and he drives Jake crazy. He kept talking to everyone on the team about pulling something for the Grudge Game, but Jake said they talked him out of it."

Very successfully, it looked like.

"When do the Stallions practice?"

"Usually a couple of times a week, but they're practicing every day to get ready for Saturday." Oscar narrowed his eyes at us. "Why?"

"Gathering the facts," I said. We thanked Oscar for the chat and started back across the cafeteria.

"Stoverton," Ivy said.

"Stoverton." I nodded. "Motive, opportunity, means—they've got it all. It's definitely an ideal Grudge Game prank."

"Okay, so they tick all the boxes, but we need more than that," Ivy said, plopping down at an empty table.

I sat beside her and we pulled out our lunches, chewing in silence.

"We have to go there," I said, a plan already forming.

"To Stoverton?"

"Yes. We have to go look for clues. Find Spartacus, if we're really lucky."

"We're never that lucky," Ivy said. "How do you plan on getting there?"

That was an excellent question. Our parents were out. We couldn't ask for help without inviting scrutiny and having to confess to violating our strict operating hours. Grantleyville had no public bus system. A cab would cost an arm and a leg. *Options, Howard, options.*

Zeroing in on the back corner, I spotted Carl sitting with Miles at a lonely table.

"I'll be right back," I called over my shoulder to Ivy. I swerved around the packed room and made my way to their spot. Despite the crowd, they had a bubble of empty chairs around them. No one wanted to associate with a suspected dognapper—aside from Miles, and I still didn't know what to make of that. Tamping down on a flare of—jealousy?—I pulled up a seat beside Carl and plopped down.

"What happened to being subtle?" he muttered around his sandwich.

"There's no time for that," I said, holding out a hand. "We've got more important things to take care of. Do you have your phone?"

"Why?" Carl frowned. Part of me admired his level of suspicion. He'd make a good P.I.

Straight shooting seemed like my best bet. "Because," I said, sitting up and looking Carl dead in the eye, "I need a ride."

Chapter Fourteen

"What do you mean you can't go to Stoverton?" I shut my locker and faced my partner, still trying to process the words coming out of her mouth.

"It's Tuesday," she said. "I have Drama Club after school."

"Why are you still going to that? You were undercover," I said. "For a case. That's closed!"

"I told you, I like it." Ivy shrugged. "And I don't want to miss the meeting. We're talking about plans for a new field trip since our other one was canceled."

"We have more important things than hobbies right now," I said, "like an active case that needs some serious legwork."

"I'm not going to drop it because you think your plans take priority," Ivy said. "Plans you made without checking with me. How was I supposed to know you were going to jump all over a Stoverton visit *today*?"

"I said—"

"*Be right back.* That's what you said. Nothing about this big brain wave." Ivy sighed. "I'm still going to work the case with you."

"Yes, that's what—"

"But I'm going to Drama Club. I'll be back on the clock tomorrow." She turned and walked down the hall, leaving me to stew. What was the point of having a partner if she wandered off whenever she felt like it?

Wait a minute. Ivy never specified when she'd be back on the clock. I didn't want to be left hanging again tomorrow morning. I jogged down the hall after her. Rounding the corner to the next hallway, I spotted her outside the door to the Drama Club room talking to Mrs. Pamuk, the club's advisor.

"I know you've got a lot on your plate," Mrs. Pamuk said to Ivy, holding out a white envelope, "but this is important. Please don't forget."

Ivy nodded and took the envelope out of Mrs. Pamuk's hands. She tucked it away in her bag, heading down the hallway. I stopped myself from calling out to her when I realized she was walking out of the building. So much for Drama Club.

Keeping my distance, I crept down the hallway after her. Two could play at the stealth game. Ivy pushed open the doors and hurried across the yard. She was already halfway down the block by the time I made it to the sidewalk. I was about to start after her when a car began honking relentlessly. Looking around for the source, I spotted Marvin parked in an alley beside the schoolyard. He rolled down the window of his ancient VW Bug and waved me over while honking a few more times for good measure.

As I walked toward Marvin's car, someone fell into step beside me. Carl. "Thought you could use some backup," he said.

Actually, not a bad idea. The Stoverton team might need some extra convincing to talk to me. Having a bruiser like Carl along for the ride could help things along. "Sounds like a plan," I said, opening up the car door. "Backup gets the backseat, though."

Footsteps pounded along the pavement, and I looked up to see Miles running over. "Hey," he said, panting. "Sorry I'm late."

"Pretty sure you can't be late to something you weren't invited to," I said.

"You said I could help." Miles frowned as he leaned on Marvin's car to catch his breath.

A sharp honk split the air, and we both jumped. "Off the car!" Marvin shouted out the window. Miles rolled his eyes but took a step away.

"I said you could help with one thing, and you did. Good job," I said. "Your cookie's in the mail."

"Not so fast," Miles said. "You need me on this. Ever been to Stoverton? Know your way around the school? Because I do. I've been there on away games."

"So has Carl," I said. We both looked over at Carl, who remained predictably silent. Miles pressed on, unwilling to let facts deter him from his argument.

"You could use an extra set of eyes," he said. "The longer you're there, the bigger risk you have of getting caught. If I help, we could be in and out."

"Some of us have better things to do with our precious time left on this earth than wait for a couple of punks to get into a dang car," Marvin hollered.

Miles shuffled his feet and looked down at me in a silent plea. It would take two of them to make up for one missing Ivy. I was going to regret this. I could feel it.

"I'm in charge," I said. "You got that?"

Miles nodded, and Marvin pulled the seat forward for Carl to climb in. "Finally," Marvin groaned. "Me and Marv Junior have been waiting forever out here."

"You named your car 'Marv Junior'?" I yanked the door shut, feeling the rattle in my teeth.

"Gen-tle! And, so? What'd you name your car? Oh, right, you don't have any wheels, and I'm doing you a favor right now by driving you."

"It's not a favor if it's for your own case, and I have Blue, thank you very much. She's just hibernating."

"Smart cookie." Marvin sat back in his seat. "Where are we headed again?"

"Marv, I told you a thousand times: Stoverton."

"Pah," Marvin spat out the window. "I was hoping you'd changed your mind. Put your seatbelt on tight; we're going to make this a quick trip."

Metal screeched as the door was yanked back open. "Leaving without me?" Leyla leaned down to glare at us, hands on her hips. She shoved my seat forward, squishing me against the dash, and scrambled into the backseat.

Marvin nodded back at her. "Friend of yours?"

"No." Leyla tucked a spike of blue hair behind her ear

and held me in a steady gaze. I gulped back the rest of my protests. “But she can stay. We’re short a pair of eyes anyway.” Maybe *three* extra pairs could make up for one.

Everyone did a quick inventory of the car. “Where’s Ivy?” Carl asked.

Excellent question. “Drama Club meeting,” I said. “Can we get this show on the road?”

“You betcha.” The engine revved as Marvin cackled.

Carl clicked his seatbelt into place and met my eyes in the rearview mirror. “You ever driven with Uncle Marv before?”

“No.”

A smirk answered my unasked question, and I was pulled back in my seat as we rocketed out onto the street. “Stoverton or bust,” Marv hollered.

-. .. -.-. -.-   .- -. -..   -. --- .-. .-

We jerked into the Stoverton Middle School parking lot and Marv Jr. spluttered to a stop. Marvin gave our surroundings a sour look. “Everybody out—this place is already giving me a rash.”

“Gimme a sec,” I said. Marvin’s warp-speed taxi service had all of my internal organs hanging onto my spine for dear life. The man took shortcuts I wasn’t sure were even technically roads.

"No puking in the car." Marvin reached across me to open the door. "Walk it off, Howard."

Carl, Leyla, Miles, and I stumbled out onto the pavement. The lot was mostly deserted. Hopefully the team was still busy with their practice and we could be in and out before anyone noticed we were there.

We slipped in through the front door, and I motioned for everyone to stay back. Miles sidled up to me. "The office is right there," he whispered. "There's a window that looks out into the hall. If anyone's in there, they'll see us right away."

Poking my head around the corner, I spotted the receptionist sitting at her desk, packing up for the day. The large window left barely enough room for us to sneak by. I ducked back to where the rest of them were still hugging the wall.

"Miles is right," I said.

He flung a hand out. "Why would I lie about that?"

"Stay low," I whispered, shooting a look at Miles. "And stay quiet."

The four of us crouched down, and we squat-walked past the office and the sign that said "ALL VISITORS MUST CHECK IN AT THE DESK." Safely in the next hallway, we straightened up and looked around. "Where to now?" Leyla asked.

Miles and Carl looked at each other.

"Left?" Miles guessed.

"Oh, for Pete's sake." I palmed my face.

Carl cocked his head to the right. "This way," he said, and jogged down the hall. The sound of bouncing basketballs grew louder as we followed him. He stopped in front of a set of closed doors that were shaking with the thumps and pounding of feet within. "Gym."

Apparently it was a good thing Carl came along. The verdict was still up in the air on the other two. "Okay, if this is the gym," I said. "The locker rooms should be close by. Let's follow our noses now."

Two doors down, we found the one marked BOYS' LOCKER ROOM. "Leyla, you keep watch," I said.

"No, no," she said, backing up down the hall. "You boys have fun. I'm in a divide-and-conquer kind of mood."

That wasn't part of my plan. This was the problem with letting other people in on a job. They got loosey-goosey with the plans. "Where are you going?"

"To do what I do best," Leyla said. "Snoop." She flashed a grin and disappeared around the corner.

"I do not feel good about this," I said to the guys.

"She gets caught, she gets caught," Carl said. "We're wasting time."

I pushed open the door and stepped inside. We each took a corner and started poking around. "What exactly are we looking for?" Miles called out.

"I don't know," I said. "We'll know it when we see it."

He shook his head. "People pay you to do this?"

"Not lately," I said, eyeballing Carl who shrugged with a small smile.

"What are you doing in here?"

We whipped around to see a Stoverton Stallions player in the doorway. So much for the luck part of the equation.

"Co-op students," I said. "Custodial co-op students. What are *you* doing in here?"

"Coach sent me for an ice pack," he said, pointing to the office in the back corner of the room. "Practice got a little rough."

"Basketball to the face?" I nodded sagely. "Been there, bro."

Carl smothered a sigh.

"That what happen to your face?" the player motioned at his eye. "Bro?"

"Hate the players, love the game," I said as Miles choked.

A smile crept across the Stallions player's face as he checked us out. "You guys are from Grantleyville. I've seen you on the team. And you're Howard Wallace, aren't you?" He pointed at me. "Bathrobe's a dead giveaway. Oscar told me you'd be coming by."

The pieces clicked. "And you're Jake," I said. "I take it Oscar filled you in?" So much for school loyalty.

"He did," Jake said, leaning up against a locker. "Rough go for you guys. If it helps, I've already questioned the team."

Unexpected. "Why would you do that?"

"Stealing another school's mascot? That's not how we operate. Or at least, it shouldn't be. I want us to win fair and square," he said, "not because we sabotaged the other side."

Rule number seven: never underestimate your opponent. I'd be playing good guy too, if I was in Jake's spot. "And you expect us to believe you?"

"Oscar told you about Chad? The one who was going to pull a prank before the game?"

"Yes," I said.

"He confessed to scoping out your school to make a plan," Jake said. "But he saw your team practicing."

"And?"

"He said pulling a prank felt mean. We're not going to need it to win."

"Oh," I said, filling in the blanks.

"Rude." Miles flopped down on a bench.

"But accurate," Carl said as he joined him.

"Want to hear my theory?" Jake grinned.

"I take it you're gonna tell us."

"Someone from your own team stole it so you'd have something to blame it on when you lose on Saturday. From what I hear, our victory's pretty much guaranteed."

Carl growled softly beside me.

"Facts are facts," Jake said. "When half of your team hates the other half, there's no way you're ever going to pull together to win—not when you're battling each other."

"Jake, how long does it take to find an ice pack?" A voice called through the door.

"That's my coach. You guys had better go," Jake said, grabbing a pack out of the cooler and jogging back toward the door. "You've got enough problems without getting caught here."

He left, and we finished taking a quick look around. There was nothing to find. The locker room was as clean as a locker room could be. I hated to admit it, but Jake may have been on to something. Time to take a closer look at the Grantleyville Gladiators.

Carl, Miles, and I snuck back out into the hallway.

"Well, that was a bust," Miles said, and I shushed him as we crept past the gym.

"Let's save the recap for the car, okay?"

"Shouldn't we at least check some closets or something?" He gestured around the hallway. "See if they have a kennel out back?"

I pressed a hand over his mouth. "Our only goal right now is to get out of here without getting caught. I think we've pressed our luck as it is."

"You're not wrong," Carl said, cocking his head toward the gym doors. The hum of the team chattering was starting to get louder. "Time to go." Carl propelled us down the hall just as the doors opened and the team spilled out of the gym.

"Aren't those Grantleyville kids?"

We didn't pause to hear the answer.

"Go, go, go," I chanted, willing my legs to move faster. Turning the corner, I spotted Leyla taking pictures of a trophy case.

"What's happening?" She took a moment to snap another picture of our frenzied race.

"Running," I said as I grabbed her arm and hauled her along with us. We booked it out of the school, bursting out onto the lawn. "Marvin," I hollered, "start the car!"

The car responded with horrible noises that I could only hope led to ignition of some sort. It roared to life as we hit the sidewalk and threw ourselves onto the seats. Somehow, Leyla finagled a spot in the front.

Marvin hit the gas, and we sped out of the parking lot, safely on the way back to Grantleyville—at least as safe as anyone riding in a tin can could be.

Everyone breathed a sigh of relief, laughing a bit as we came down off the adrenaline rush.

"That was amazing," Miles said. "That was so awesome." He held up his hands for high fives which I refused to dignify. Carl rolled his eyes, but indulged him in the gesture. "Yeah." Miles reached a hand into the front seat causing Marvin to curl a lip.

"Put your hand down, son."

I pushed Miles back and leaned forward to peer at Leyla. "How'd it go on your end? Find anything?"

"Not sure yet," Leyla said, pursing her lips. "Got a thread to tug. How about you guys?"

"We ruled out some possibilities."

Leyla leveled a look at the backseat. "So . . . nothing?"

"I mean, we might not have Spartacus, but we found out some stuff," Miles said. "And ran for our lives, which was cool."

"Calm down," I said. "Nobody was running for their lives. We wouldn't have had to run at all if you'd listened and left when I said we should go."

"Ah, it all worked out fine."

"Not the point." I twisted around to glare at him. "The rule was that I was in charge. You agreed to that and didn't follow through."

"Howard, chill," Miles said. "Lesson learned for next time."

This is what I got for working with amateurs. I didn't want there to be a next time.

I needed my partner back.

Chapter Fifteen

Marvin offered to take me home, but I had one more stop on my list. He dropped me off in front of Ivy's place.

"See you tomorrow," Miles called out, and I slammed the door to cut him off.

"Door!" Marvin shouted.

"Sorry, Marv." I waved as he peeled away from the curb. Then I paced the sidewalk for a few minutes, debating what to say to Ivy. Deep in the pit of my stomach sparked a small seed of doubt. What she did on her own time wasn't really any of my business.

But lying about it?

If we were partners, there was no room for lies between

us. That was part of the deal. Squaring my shoulders, I marched up to her front door and knocked on the wood.

No answer.

I took another crack at the door, and it swung inward. Ivy stood there, wild-haired and red-faced, in head-to-toe flannel. "You trying to break the door down?" She leaned an elbow on the doorframe, leveling a look at me.

I stepped through the door and scraped my boots on the mat. "How was Drama Club?"

"Fine," she said. "How was—don't-you-dare-spit-when-I-say-it—Stoverton?"

"I don't know if I'd call it a dead end, but it didn't crack the case either." I unzipped my coat and let my bag fall to the floor. Ivy's house was roasting. "We met Jake, the other captain."

"Who's 'we'?"

"Me, Carl, Leyla, and Miles," I said. "Well, Leyla didn't meet him. She was off doing—I have no idea what."

"Tight crew you're running there."

"I did the best I could under partnerless circumstances. What'd you do in Drama Club today?"

"Why'd you let Miles go with you to Stoverton?"

This game could go on forever, and after today I wasn't in the mood for running in circles—or for any kind of running, for that matter.

"Miles came along because he was familiar with the school, he wanted to help, and he was actually there to do so." I ticked off my answers on one hand.

"So, Miles comes back around and you're suddenly falling all over yourself to include him? What happened to 'he is evil and we do not speak his name'?"

"It's just for the case, Ivy." I ground out the words. "Tell me about Drama Club."

"Why the sudden interest?" She played with the ends of her hair, separating the curls. "I've been going for months, and you usually pretend it doesn't exist."

"I saw you leave." It came out in a blurt.

The clock by the door ticked off the seconds it took for Ivy to process that. "You *followed* me?"

"*No*," I said. "I was looking for you where you were supposed to be and found you bailing instead."

"I didn't feel well, okay?" She scrubbed a hand over her face. "I thought you'd already left. I wouldn't have been any help anyway, so I went home. End of story."

Except it wasn't. The scene with Mrs. Pamuk played

through my brain, twisting over until it fit with a click that didn't sit well at all. One that involved the worst kind of betrayal.

"What was in the envelope?"

"What envel—are you serious, right now?" Ivy flopped down onto the coatrack bench. "Howard, please stop."

"Did you take on a case without me?" The question was out before I realized I'd been thinking it. Ivy looked up and hit me with a dead-eyed stare. She grabbed her backpack up off the floor and fished through it. Wordlessly, she handed me a white envelope.

I held on, not quite ready to open it.

"Go ahead," Ivy said. "Read away."

Pulling back the flap, I tugged the paper out of the envelope. My cheeks flamed as I skimmed the words. "A permission slip," I said, "to be in the spring musical."

"Yup." Ivy held open her bag, flashing papers and another crumpled envelope at me. "I've got more good stuff in here. You want to keep going?"

"No," I said. "You can be in the play, you know. You didn't have to hide this."

"First of all," Ivy said, standing up and waving a finger in the air, "I wasn't hiding it. Second of all—no, wait. Make this one first of all. First of all, again, I don't need your permission to do anything."

"You're right." I handed the paper and envelope back to her. "And I'm sorry."

"I'm not Miles, okay?" Ivy stuffed everything back in her bag and chucked it on the floor. "I'm not going to get weird and abandon you. Dial down the paranoia."

"This stupid case is getting to me," I said, sinking down to the floor.

"I think hanging out with Miles is getting to you," Ivy said as she joined me and leaned back against the wall.

"It was actually not one hundred percent horrible working with him today," I said. "It was like falling back into an old habit."

"Which makes you mad because you're mad at him, so now you're double-mad."

I looked at my partner as I unpacked that statement. "Yeah," I said. "Exactly. Part of me wants to let it all go—"

"But you don't trust him," Ivy finished for me.

I shook my head. "Not even a little bit."

"Well, Howard, here's what I think . . ." she began.

Cupping my hands around my head, I leaned in.

"What are you doing?" Ivy frowned.

"Got my listening ears on."

She batted my hands away. "I've got my serious face on, so stop being a goof." Ivy poked a finger at my chest. "I think if someone hurt you, then the only person who can decide if they should be allowed back into your life is you."

I mulled that over. "You are very wise, partner of mine."

"Yes, I am." Ivy laughed thickly and rubbed at her nose. She actually didn't look all the great. I reached into my pocket to offer her a piece of Juicy. "You okay?"

"I'm fine," she said, waving away the gum. "Having an off day."

The front door opened, and Ivy's grandma stepped in. She stopped short at the sight of us hanging out on the floor of the entryway. "Hello, Howard," she said. "Are you staying for dinner?"

I caught the look that crossed between Ivy and her grandma. Let it never be said that I couldn't read a room. "No, thanks, Lillian," I said. "I've got to get home. See you tomorrow morning, Ivy?"

She nodded. "Bright and early."

Bundling back up, I let myself out and started down the street. Part of me was glad to have sorted things out with Ivy, but I couldn't shake the feeling that my partner still wasn't telling me everything.

Chapter Sixteen

Wednesday morning, I stood on the corner waiting. Again. Luckily, irritation at my absent partner kept me warm from the inside out. "What the heck, Ivy," I muttered. "Where are you?"

"Howard!"

I turned and spotted Miles half a block back. He waved as he ran over, reaching me before I'd finished debating whether or not to wave back.

"Hey," he said. "I was hoping I'd catch you here."

"Why?"

"To work on the case?"

The case that I was supposed to be working with my

partner. Perhaps it was time to revisit the punctuality portion of Ivy's training.

I started off toward the school. "I let you help out yesterday," I said to Miles. "I didn't say anything about today."

Miles shrugged into his coat against the biting wind. "Come on, Howard," he said. "You still need me."

I sneered at that, reaching inside my jacket to pull up the collar of my lucky coat. "I think I'll get by."

"We're back on home turf, right? You're looking at the team again." Miles pulled ahead so he could walk backward and face me. "Half of those guys won't talk to Carl. Most of them won't talk to you, no matter what Coach says. I'm your in."

Something told me I was better off testing that theory than taking Miles's word for it.

"I could probably get them to open their lockers for you, too," he said.

"Well, now you're taking all the fun out of it," I said.

Miles snickered as I rolled my eyes. "Come on," he said. "What's your rule thing? 'Work with what you've got'?"

I shot him a sharp look and he held up his hands. "What? Is it a secret? You mutter about it all the time," he said. "Sometimes I pay attention."

I shoved my hands into my pockets, uncomfortable with how much Miles seemed to have picked up about our operation. He pressed on, eager to make his case.

"It's your rule number one, right? You need to make use of every resource," he said, warming up to the topic. "And in this case, I'm pretty much number one. Without me, you've got nothing."

"Hey, Fletcher! Fletcher! Over here!"

The shouts pulled Miles out of his pitch as he looked around for the source. Two guys stood at the corner of the street. Miles's wide smile dropped off and I stiffened as we recognized Vince and another teammate. Miles stood frozen in place; his eyes darted between me and his still shouting friends.

"'*I'm your in,*'" I parroted back to Miles. "'*You need my help. I can get them to talk to you.*'"

"Yeah, I know," he said as the guys headed our way. "Gimme a sec to figure this out."

"Hey, didn't you hear us? I thought I was going to bust a lung yelling for you," Vince said, ambling up to us, an easy smile on his face. My stomach did a slow slide as I remembered how easily that smile could turn into something dangerous. The image of it glinting at me had been seared into my brain since last March when he stuffed me in my locker, refusing to let me out until Pete the custodian broke up the crowd. It was the first time Miles had joined in, helping to slam the door in my face.

Good times.

I shook my brain clear of the memories and focused on the task at hand. Dealing with the team was a necessary evil, and if Miles could help speed up that process, I wasn't going to turn him down. Waiting for my opening, I watched as Miles and the guys exchanged a complicated series of handshakes. The shorter guy shuffling along behind Vince was Devon. He never actively participated in my torment, but he liked to watch. The metal walls of a locker didn't do much to muffle his laughter.

"What are you doing, man?" Vince punched at Miles's side. "You don't walk this way to school."

"I was talking to Howard about Spartacus," Miles said. "Seeing how the case is going."

"Found him yet?" Devon turned to me, his smile fading. "We need him for Saturday. It's not looking good for us. We need Sparty."

I shook my head to clear it of the bizarre sensation of actually having a conversation with these guys. "I'm following some leads," I said. "Since you're here, I have some ques—"

"Hold up. What is this?" Vince's hand shot out to grab

the collar of my lucky coat, tugging it loose from the confines of my winter jacket. "Are you wearing a *bathrobe*?"

Vince and Devon burst out laughing while Miles shifted on his feet, focusing on the sidewalk.

"He always wears it," Devon said. "Remember when he couldn't get out of the locker because he had so many layers on?"

"Oh, yeah! I almost forgot about that." Vince snorted.

Taking a breath to steady myself, I pulled a notebook out of my pocket. "Okay, enough with the yuks," I said. "About the case—"

"Miles, this kid is so weird," Vince said, shaking his head. "I can't believe you guys used to hang out."

We all turned to face Miles, waiting for a response. He kept communing with sidewalk.

"Howeird." It was uttered so faintly I thought maybe it was a trick of the wind.

"I'm sorry, what?" Vince leaned in to Miles, rolling up onto his toes.

Miles cleared his throat. "His sister calls him Howeird," he said, glancing over at the guys.

"Howeird?" Vince crowed. "Ho*weird*? That is the best. I'm stealing it."

"Shut up," I said. "You don't get to call me that." I fired off a look at Miles. "None of you get to call me that."

"You don't get a vote, Howeird." Vince laughed.

My hands curled into fists as I glared at the three of them. Vince and Devon cracking up. Miles looking everywhere and anywhere but at me. "In case you've forgotten, I'm the one doing you a favor here, trying to find Spartacus so you can pretend your lousy team has a chance this year."

That did the trick. Their mouths snapped shut and Vince stepped forward. "Listen up, Howeird," he said and Miles put a hand on his shoulder.

"No worries," Miles said. "I've got this." He leaned over, getting right in my face, finally looking me in the eyes. "Howard," he said. "I think you need to cool off." With one hand, he shoved against my chest, toppling me over into the snowbank. I landed with a thud, and the three of them were off laughing again.

"See you later, Howeird," Vince called as they walked away.

I let my head flop back into the snowbank and huffed out a breath. I wanted to be shocked, but I wasn't even a little bit surprised—except maybe for the level of my own idiocy.

Of course I was lying in a snowbank right now. Of course I was. I should never have let Miles get within breathing distance of me and this case. I got sucked in when I knew better. How could I think for one second that Miles was anything but a liar and a fake?

I lay there in the snow, temper cooling as the wheels started turning.

A liar.

And a fake.

And right in the middle of my investigation.

Footsteps approached, and I raised my head to see Miles hurrying down the sidewalk. Back for round two. "Sorry, Howard," he said. "It took me a little bit to lose them so I could come back."

"To finish the job?"

"What? No, to help you . . . ," he said, like it made the most sense in the world, "out of here." He gestured vaguely at where I was splayed out. "And to work the case. Like we were talking about."

"*You* pushed me here." I slapped away his outstretched hands. I might not look graceful hauling myself out of the pile, but there was no way I was accepting Miles's assistance. "You told them Eileen's stupid nickname," I snapped. "In what universe is that helpful?"

Miles sputtered as I stumbled onto the sidewalk. Sodden pants and a frozen behind did nothing to quell the growing fire in my gut.

"Okay, I get it," he said. "Sorry I pushed you, but if I didn't do something, you would've gotten worse from them."

Swatting the snow off my sides, I grunted. "I sincerely hope you're not looking for a thank-you."

Miles shrugged and looked away.

"Oh." The scoff popped out before I could stop it. "Well, don't hold your breath waiting for it." I pushed my way past him and started toward the school. After a beat, I heard the sound of his boots falling in line beside me.

"Can we put this aside and work on the case?"

Without missing a step, I glanced over at him, a bright fleck on the shoulder of his coat catching my eye. I'd never stopped working the case. "Sure," I said. "Let's do that. Where were you last Tuesday night?"

Miles laughter faded away as I whipped out my notebook from my pocket. "What are you doing?" he asked. "You already interviewed me."

"No, I didn't," I said, tapping the side of my still-tender nose. "We were interrupted, remember?"

His cheeks colored faintly at the memory and he tugged at his hat. “I was at home,” he muttered.

“Can anyone verify that?” I held a pencil over the page.

Miles spotted my ready stance and rolled his eyes. “My family.”

“They were with you the whole night?”

“No, Howard. I was alone in my room doing homewo—this is ridiculous, why am I even entertaining this?”

“You wanted to help. Unless you have something to hide?”

“No. Why don’t you just ask me if I took the dumb dog and get it over with?”

“Why’d you say that?” I halted our progress by stepping in front of him.

“Say what?”

“Why’d you call Spartacus a dumb dog? Did you not get along?”

“He’s a dog. It’s not like we had a deep relationship.” Miles shuffled on the spot, trying to warm up his patch of sidewalk. “Look, everyone likes Spartacus,” he said. “He’s basically a basketball with fur, but he’s a good dog.”

“Did you take him?”

“No, Howard,” Miles said, meeting my eyes. “I did not take Spartacus. Trust me; our team could use a good-luck charm right now. Any other questions?”

Why did you laugh?

Why did you leave?

Why bother coming back?

"No," I said, shoving my notebook back into the recesses of my coat. "We're done."

"Good. Okay." Miles nodded. "So, where are we starting—"

"No, Miles," I cut him off swiftly. "We're done here. You're not helping anymore. I've got it from here."

His eyebrows slammed together as he processed that. "Howard, come on. You're being ridiculous."

"It's nothing personal," I said. "Strictly business. We're running out of time. I need to streamline the process and cut some of the deadweight."

Miles worked his jaw as he bit back a reply and stared back at me hard. "Fine," he eventually ground out. "Be that way." He swept past me, and I plucked the shiny fleck off his shoulder as he went by.

Now I'm the liar, I thought as I examined the short, golden strand in the sunlight. We weren't done. I pulled out my notebook and carefully rolled up the dog hair in a piece of paper, tucking it back inside.

Not done by a long shot.

Chapter Seventeen

"What do you mean, 'Miles is the dognapper'?"

Ivy and I had collided in a flurry of limbs at the front of the school. I'd waved away her apologies for being late. We had bigger fish to fry.

"Slow down, Howard." My partner rubbed at her forehead with a sigh. "I'm gonna need you to fill in some blanks here."

I quickly broke down the morning's events with Miles, Vince, and Devon. Ivy scrunched up her face as she processed. "And who are Vince and Devon, again?"

"They're on the team," I said, pulling on the last of my patience.

"Okay," she said. "There are *far* too many basketball

players involved in this case. How big does a team need to be, anyway? There's only one ball."

"Ivy, focus."

"Fine, fine, fine." She flipped open her notebook to doodle out some notes. "So how does this end up with Miles as the dognapper?"

"The facts are these," I said. "Miles wormed his way into the case practically from day one. Why? To get an inside track and see how much we know. Why else would he keep pushing? He's digging, trying to stay one step ahead. He doesn't have a solid alibi. And to top it off . . ." I pulled the notebook out of my pocket and unfolded the page of evidence to show Ivy.

"Dog hair," I said. "Miles doesn't have any pets."

"Right," Ivy said, examining the strand. "Hold your 'ahas' for a minute. This is not what I would call an airtight solution."

I snatched back the book and held it tight as we headed into the school. "We've got sketchy behavior, plenty of opportunity, a dubious alibi, and physical evidence."

"You can't count the hair as evidence," Ivy protested. "Miles could have a dog you don't know about. It's not like you've been keeping up with each other's lives."

I threw a scowl at her as I marched up to my locker. "I thought you'd be happy to have this case in the bag."

Ivy leaned up against the wall of lockers and sighed. "I would be," she said. "But I think 'in the bag' is a bit of a stretch. Just because Miles is a creep doesn't mean we can keep him at the top of our suspect list. We still have other leads that need to be eliminated. We can't go tearing off without more to go on. What about motive?" She tossed her hands up at that.

"Aha!" I said and she rolled her eyes. "I have a hunch about that. Come on." I tossed my stuff in the locker and slammed it shut. Grabbing my partner's hand, I tugged her down the hall. We fought against a sea of kids spilling out of the music room at the end of the corridor. When my quarry didn't emerge, I nudged Ivy into the room.

"Oh, hi guys!" Scotty was gathering up sheets of music from the stands around the room. "You just missed practice. Band's sounding pretty good this year, if I do say so myself."

"That's great," I said, pulling the pages out of his hands and dumping them on a desk. Ivy directed him into a chair, and we huddled up in front of him. "Listen, Scotty, we need some help with this case. Mind answering a couple of questions for us?"

"Oh yeah, sure, for sure." Scotty nodded vigorously. "Anything for Spartacus. And the team."

"Perfect," I said. "We appreciate it." The first bell rang, and Ivy motioned for me to move it along.

"If Oscar ends up moving to Stoverton, who's next in line to be captain of the team?"

Scotty reflected on that and sniffed. "Well, technically it'd be up to Coach, so he'd probably stick us with a Grantley. If we were doing things the right way, my first guess would be Carl. He's the second-best player on the team, and he's one of the seniors. But—"

I nodded for him to continue.

"That was before everything went bananas. I don't know if he's permanently off the team or not," he said. "If I went with the best player after Carl, I'd probably have to say Miles?"

"Is that a question or a statement?" I drummed my fingers against my leg, itching for answers.

"Mmmmm." Scotty wiped at his nose and pondered a moment more. I needed to expand my pool of sources. Find me some fast talkers. "Definitely," he finally said. "Definitely Miles."

"Okay, great," I said, dragging Ivy with me backward out into the hall. "Thanks for your time, Scotty. Appreciate it."

We ran over to Ivy's locker so she could stash her things.

"See? Miles brings Spartacus back, he's a big hero—boom, team captain," I said, rocking back on my heels. "Motive."

"Oh, hang on," Ivy said as she peered at me from around the metal door. "You've got something right there." She wiped at my chin. "Bit of smug."

I smirked, and she rubbed harder. "Uh-oh. I think it might be permanent."

Ducking out of her grip, I landed right back on my point. "You have to admit that this is worth looking into."

Ivy bobbed her head as she drew in a breath. "Yeeeeessss," she said. "It'd be so much better if it was Stoverton instead."

"Why?"

"It's disappointing when people live up to your lowest opinion of them," Ivy said, closing up her locker and starting toward class, "even if you're expecting it."

"You should start getting used to that in our line of work," I said.

"So, how do we go about this? What's the plan?"

I'd been working on that since my swan dive into the snow this morning. "Stakeout."

"Jumping right to stakeout?" Ivy shot me a look. "Bit extreme. Why don't we start with searching his locker?"

"We're not going to find Spartacus in his locker." At least, I hoped not. "We need absolute proof to wrap this up, and that means finding Miles red-pawed."

"Terrible jokes won't cover the fact that this feels risky." My partner poked at me with an elbow, and I started to bristle at her doubts.

"Maybe that's because you haven't been taking any of the risks this week?"

"Okay. Rude."

"I'm just saying. Who's the one who almost got caught at Stoverton?" I tugged on my collar. "Me. As in: the person who has been doing the bulk of the investigating."

Ivy set her jaw, frowning. "I've been helping."

"Yes, you were an awesome help this morning when you were not meeting me on time."

"My phone died." Ivy shoved at my arm. "My alarm didn't go off, and I had to get another ride with my grandma." She played with the ends of her hair, and I shook my head at how easily the lie fell from her lips. I wondered if she knew she had a tell. "I'm sorry I was late again. I'm having an off week."

That was an understatement. "Tell me about it," I said.

"Well—"

"Between Marvin, Mr. Williams, and Miles," I ticked them

off on my fingers, "we've been up to our ears in it." I turned back as she fell behind. "In any case, you could have called."

Her head shot up at that. "Did your parents give you your phone back yet?" She nodded sagely at my silence. "Exactly."

"That's beside the point. Anyway, I'm deeper in this mess than you, so I get to decide, and I say 'stakeout.' "

"Howard."

"Stake. Out."

Ivy sighed. "When do you want to do this?"

"After school," I said, already mapping out the perfect spot.

"Today?" My partner squeaked.

"No, next week," I said. "After he's had time to carry out his evil plan and conceal all evidence of a crime. Yes, today." Ivy's frown put a hitch in my plans. "Why?"

"I have a thing after school," she said, head down, toeing at a crack in the tile floor.

"Like what?" Ivy's things were hanging out with me and, for whatever inexplicable reason, Drama Club. By my calculations, she should be free and clear. "This is home stretch, Ivy. You want to miss out on closing the case? What's going on?"

"Nothing." Ivy shook her head and looked up with half a smile. "My dad wanted me to do some stuff, but it can wait."

"Are you sure?" I poked at her side. "I mean, I could try asking Miles to move any incriminating acts to tomorrow."

"Quit it." Ivy swatted at my hand. "Today's fine. I can't leave my idiot partner to pull this off on his own."

"Hey—" She cut off my retort to pull me out of the way as someone rushed by, narrowly missing a collision. We both watched as Leyla continued down the hall, arms so full of yearbooks she hadn't even noticed us. "I'm in, but if we're going through with this," Ivy pointed after her and shot me a look, "we need backup."

Chapter Eighteen

We found Carl and Leyla during lunch to get them up to speed. "It'd be better if we could talk somewhere private," I said, scanning the bustling cafeteria. "For Carl's sake."

Carl kept his gratitude to himself.

"I've got a place." Leyla jerked her head toward the hallway. "Hang on."

She left the caf and came back a few minutes later, slightly out breath. "Okay, follow me." Leyla led us down the hall and stopped in front of one of Pete's supply closets. "In here."

"It's locked," I said. Pete kept things running smoothly around the school, everything in its proper place, locked up as it should be—unless I happened to slide him his favorite bribe: a fresh six-pack of doughnuts. Which I had neglected to do. I racked my brain for an alternate location.

Leyla hauled the door open and grinned. "Not if the price is right."

My eyes and ears were deceiving me. Ivy pushed me into the closet after tapping my chin back up in place. "Let's get down to business," she said.

"Yes," I said, turning to Leyla as she shut the door behind us. "How'd you get us in here?"

"Pete lets me use the closet when I need it," she said.

"I think this is off-topic, Howard," Ivy said.

"It's the only topic right now," I said. "What do you mean, Pete lets you use this closet?"

Leyla shrugged. "I bring him homemade treats. What's a little bribe between friends?"

My mouth opened and closed, unable to form the words to fully comprehend this betrayal.

"Seriously?" Ivy said. "You're surprised that a dude who takes bribes from a middle schooler takes bribes from more than one middle schooler?"

"It's the principle of the thing."

Carl set a bucket upside down in the corner and took a seat. "Let me know when we get to the point."

Right. The point. Scrutinizing Pete's duplicitous nature would have to wait. We had a stakeout to plan. "I've got a suspect for Spartacus's kidnapping," I said as Leyla and Carl perked up. Ivy pursed her lips.

"Don't get excited until he tells you who it is," she said.

"After carefully narrowing down the field," I said, shooting Ivy a look when she coughed. "I've concluded that Miles Fletcher is a person of interest in this case."

"Miles." Carl sat up straight. "Why?"

"He had the means, motive, and opportunity."

Carl shook his head. "He's my friend."

"You're not the first person to think that," I said.

"He told me to put his name on the suspect list," Carl pointed out.

"An excellent diversion tactic, don't you think? Makes it look like he's being up front," I said. "When he's really going behind our backs."

The closet was silent as Carl and Leyla absorbed this new development. I dug two granola bars out of my pocket and tossed one to Ivy. Might as well enjoy the lunch part of our working lunch.

Leyla leaned back against the door. "What kind of motive?"

"Paving the way to be captain of the team," I said around a mouthful of oats.

"But," Carl said, "it's not for sure that Oscar's leaving."

"That's where his plan is kind of genius." I quickly swallowed before continuing. "Miles has lost playing time, right?"

"Yeah," Carl said. "He's not the only one, though."

"Right, but not everyone is going to get that time back. Even if things don't fall into place for Miles to get captain, he's still going to come out on top." Wheels were spinning furiously as I walked myself through Miles's possible plans. "He takes Spartacus and everyone's upset. The team is in an uproar. All he has to do is cool his heels till Saturday, show up with the dog, be the hero, and Mr. Williams will be so grateful, he'll have him starting again."

"In theory," Leyla said.

"Mr. Williams is climbing the walls enough that I could see it playing out that way," Ivy said. I nodded at my partner, grateful for the backup.

"As much as I'm enjoying this quality time together," Leyla said, "let's cut to the chase. You've made some good guesses, but how do you plan to get proof?" Carl broadcast his own doubts with a single side-eyed glance.

“Easy,” I said. “We catch him in the act. Stakeout. Today after school.”

“I don’t like it.” Carl stood, cracking his neck. “But nothing else has panned out. Don’t have any other options at this point.”

“I reserve the right to record everything,” Leyla said, whisking out her phone and starting to jot down the plan in her schedule.

“That’s pretty much understood at this point, Leyla.” I sighed. We’d figure out how to get the footage off her later.

“So, we’re really doing this?” Carl tapped on the shelves, eager to get out of our cramped quarters. “Spying on Miles?”

“It’s not spying—it’s gathering evidence.” A slight, but important difference. I laid out the plan and made sure everyone was clear on their roles. As soon as school was over, we could put things in motion.

Chapter Nineteen

The bell rang, and Ivy and I raced to our lockers. We had to beat Miles out of school if our plan was going to work. Grabbing our bags, we busted our way through the crowd and out the doors.

Ivy and I huffed and puffed our way down the sidewalk. "I still think we're getting ahead of ourselves," she said between gasps. "We need to clear the rest of the team, you could have missed something at Stoverton—"

"Uh, how would you know if we missed anything at Stoverton?" I shot her a sideways glance. "That was some of my finest investigative work, I'll have you know."

"I thought you got caught by one of the players."

"Who I then tricked into giving me information."

"Okay, fine," she said. "I'm saying I think we shouldn't rule out other avenues of investigation. And I don't want you to be disappointed if this stakeout doesn't turn up anything."

We slowed our pace as we drew nearer to Miles's house. "Oh, it will."

Our plan was simple: Leyla and Carl were following Miles home, and they were to take the front-yard watch, setting up their post on a park bench across the street. Ivy and I had gone ahead so we could set up in the backyard. There was a hedge of evergreens that would provide us with ample coverage and a clear view of the back of the house. When Miles brought Spartacus outside to do his business, *we'd* be in business.

"I'm freezing," Ivy said.

"We just got here."

"I know." She blew on her mittens. "My enthusiasm for this plan is plummeting. Do you really want to freeze to death for a stakeout?"

"Wouldn't be the worst way to go out."

Ivy cackled and scooted closer to me. "I'm stealing all of your warmth, so you bite it first."

"Never going to happen," I said, pulling the corner of my lucky coat out of my sleeve. "You gotta learn to dress in layers. I came prepared."

My partner snuggled in, tugging part of my terrycloth sleeve over her mitts. She finally sat still. Too still. I could feel the questions pressing against my personal space bubble.

"What?" I looked over at her. "Spill."

"Do you want it to be Miles?" It came out in a rush, like those weren't the words she was expecting to say.

"I don't want it to be anybody," I said. "I'd like Spartacus to be home safe and for us to be working cases where people actually pay us."

"No, I mean . . . ," Ivy stumbled over her next thought, "will you be happy if it's him and he gets into trouble?"

"Not happy," I said, digging into the hard ground with the toe of my shoe. *Happy* definitely wasn't what I would classify it as. *Vindicated*?

"It's complicated," I said. "Last year was ten pounds of garbage in a five-pound bag. That's all there is to it. This year, it seemed like we were mostly leaving each other alone. I had you and the agency. Miles and I haven't run into each other all that much. I didn't forget, but it was—"

"Easier," Ivy supplied.

"Yeah." I nodded at that. "But then this case and now it's not—easy."

Ivy made a sympathetic noise that was quickly overpowered by the gurgling of her stomach. "We really need to stop working through lunch," she said, laughing.

"Crime doesn't stop for meals," I shot back.

A rustling noise brought the conversation to a halt. Ivy and I froze as we waited for the intruder to appear.

"You guys hungry?" Miles dragged branches aside and held out a bag full of granola bars.

Ivy grabbed the bag out of his hands. "Oooh, snacks," she said, digging through the selection.

"What are you doing?" I snatched the bag from Ivy and tossed it back to Miles. Things had gone spectacularly sideways. "Get out of here. You're not supposed to be—how—"

"How are you supposed to spy on me when I'm right here?" Miles fished out a granola bar and lobbed it over to Ivy.

She wavered a look between me and the food in her hand. "It's not spying," she said finally, chucking the bar at Miles's feet. "It's a stakeout. Don't think you get to argue about it after your little show this morning."

Miles huffed as he reached down to tuck the granola bar back into his bag. "Fine," he said. "Whatever. What do you want?"

"You got any dogs in there?" She peered over Miles's shoulder into the backyard.

"I do, actually," Miles said. "His name is Archer. Want to meet him?"

I scowled at them both. Our covert operation had been blown wide open and they were acting like this was a trip to the dog park.

"Yes," Ivy said as I shook my head no. She took me aside for a whispered consultation. "Howard, the stakeout's a bust. Let's get the answers we need. See if this dog is who Miles says he is."

"What?" Miles leaned in, not bothering to hide his eaves-dropping. "You think it's Spartacus in a retriever costume?"

Ivy cracked a smile. "You'd have to put him on stilts to make that work."

"Stop it," I said. "Both of you." I turned to Ivy. "This is a serious investigation. Could you please act like it?"

"Don't yell at her," Miles said, frowning.

"I can speak for myself," Ivy said, scrambling out of the bushes. "And I also say, 'Stop yelling at me.' "

Crawling out after her, I stood up and brushed off my coat. "I'm not yelling. I just don't appreciate you palling around with a suspect."

Ivy held up a hand. "I'm not 'palling around' with any-one," she said. "You don't need to jump all over me for a little joke. Especially when it's clear there's nothing here. Can we leave now?"

"Not a chance," I said, turning to Miles. "Show us this dog."

Miles spun back around and strode over to the back door of his house. "Here, boy!" he called, after opening the door a crack. A golden ball of fluff plowed into him, and Miles stumbled backward, barely getting a hand around its collar. We watched as he got control of the wriggling beast. "Archer, meet Ivy and Howard." Archer barked once then let his mouth hang open in a giant grin, pink tongue hanging over the edge.

All of my theories danced away, moving farther out of reach. "This doesn't prove anything," I said. "How do we know you don't have Spartacus inside?"

"Howard," Ivy said softly, and Miles went still.

"Do you want to search my house? Poke around until you find what you're looking for? Is there a prewritten confession you'd like me to sign? Seems like you've already decided how you want this to go," Miles snapped. Archer whined, and Miles gently nudged him back inside the house. He turned back to us. "Are you done with this fishing expedition?"

Ivy pulled on my sleeve. "We should go."

"Go then." I shrugged her off. "It's what you've been doing all this week. I'm trying to solve this case. For some reason, I'm the only one making an effort."

"Railroading Miles is not solving the case, Howard," she said. "It's revenge, and I'm done with it." Ivy picked up her bag and left.

"Do you really hate me that much, Howard?" Miles asked quietly.

I rubbed at my forehead, unable to untangle the answer to that question.

"What's it going to take? What can I say to get you to let some of this go?"

"This has nothing to do with you. It's about the case."

Miles stared at me and slowly shook his head. "Right."

I wanted to find Spartacus and be done with this mess. It really wasn't that much to ask. "It's called 'chasing down a lead,' Miles," I said. "It's not personal. Try and get over yourself."

"I will when you stop lying to yourself. Admit it. You'd have been thrilled to find Spartacus here and get the chance to turn me in."

I stared him down, not about to admit anything. Any lie could become the truth if you said it enough.

He ran a hand over his face. "Listen, I meant what I said about wanting to help. I'm sorry about this morning. I don't know what else you want—"

"What I want?" I exploded. "How about standing up for me for once? Why is joining in on the torture your first choice? What's so hard about saying no?"

Miles shoved his hands into his pockets, refusing to meet my eyes. There was a small thump as Archer pressed his face into the back window, concern for the humans oozing out of every pore. Ivy was right. I should have gotten out of here a long time ago. I turned to leave and almost missed Miles's soft response.

"Not everyone's as brave as you."

"Don't give me that," I said. "You don't get to cop out on this."

"You've got a good friend in Ivy, you know." He finally looked up and a tiny smile flit across his face. "You should listen to her. Apologize, maybe."

"Ivy and I are fine," I said. "Also, pretty sure you're the last person I should take advice from."

Miles shrugged, buttoning up his sweater against the wind. "Just trying to help."

"It's funny," I said. "You helping still looks an awful lot like you messing up my life."

"Fine," he said. "I'm out. Make sure you tell Carl it wasn't me. Good luck with the rest of it." The door slammed behind him, and I could hear Archer barking like crazy at the sound.

Grabbing my bag, I trudged around the side of the house, back out to the sidewalk. Leyla and Carl were waiting.

"We saw Ivy go," Leyla said. "Did you find Spartacus? Was it Miles? What's going on?"

I shook my head. "Negative across the board."

"That's good," Carl said, surprising us both with that statement. "I mean, bad you didn't find Spartacus, but I'm glad—glad it's not Miles."

We made plans to meet up again the next day and went our separate ways. I couldn't find it in my heart to be glad it wasn't Miles. That particular organ was too full of dread over the fact that we were back to square one—worse than square one. Our leads were crumbling, the trail was growing cold, and I had no idea where my partner had run off to.

Of the three, that last one had me worried the most.

Chapter Twenty

I woke up on Thursday morning with an aching head and the taste of bitter words still on my tongue. It had been too late to stop by Ivy's house last night, and she hadn't picked up any of my calls. Tracking down new leads was job number one today, but I couldn't do that without my partner. Time to do something about that. Grabbing a shirt out of the pile on the floor, I gave it a sniff and pulled it on. No more waiting on the sidewalk for Ivy. This time, I was going to her.

I stopped by the garage to say hi to Blue. Winters were pretty lonely for the old girl. I adjusted her blankets and checked on her tire pressure, listening to her creaks and groans as she settled in. "Atta girl, Blue." I gave her a pat before heading out. Nice to be sure of one person in my corner.

Setting out on foot, I made my way over to Ivy's house. I was halfway up the walk when Ivy's door opened and she came storming out. "I don't *have* to do anything," she yelled, pulling on her hat and bag.

Her grandmother appeared in the doorway behind her. "We're not done talking about this, Ivy." She reached out, cupping Ivy's cheek in her hand. "It's important to talk about it."

Ivy jerked her head away. "I need to get to school. I don't want to be late." She ran down the steps, calling out a quick good-bye. Barreling down the driveway, Ivy stopped short at the sight of me, waiting there for her.

"What are you doing here?"

I waved at Lillian, who was keeping an eye on us from the front stoop. "I wanted to talk to you."

Ivy squared her backpack on her shoulders and started on a brisk march up the sidewalk. "So, talk," she said.

I sped up to keep pace with her. "I shouldn't have yelled at you yesterday," I said.

"Are we going to talk about something I don't already know?"

"How about, 'I'm sorry'?" I stepped in front of Ivy so we could be face to face. "I am," I said. "I'm really sorry."

She eyed me warily. "Are you all done with the Miles

thing? No more making your theories fit the case?"

"I was following logical clues," I said, bristling at her tone. "It's our job to check out every lead."

"Oh, man," she said. "Would it kill you to admit that that wasn't the best call?"

"Partners are supposed to back each other up."

"Not when one of them is going off on half-baked vendettas. I know you and Miles have a history—"

"I was following the clues. They led to Miles. That's all there is to it."

"Howard, I'm trying to be supportive, but that doesn't mean I'm going to blindly follow you while you do whatever you want," she said. "That's not what a partnership is, remember?"

"It's a little hard to tell lately," I snapped, starting back up the sidewalk.

"What is that supposed to mean?" Ivy said, chasing after me.

"The disappearing, the arguing." The lying. "Feels more like I've been running a solo operation lately."

"I'm sorry you feel that way."

"What was going on with your grandma back there?

"What?"

"It looked like you were fighting."

"Oh," Ivy said, pulling apart a lock of her hair and twirling it on her fingers. "I told her about yesterday, and she was trying to get me to talk to you about it. Thought we should make up."

"Ah," I said, watching her out of the corner of my eye. Lying. Again. "Well, it's not a bad suggestion. In theory."

"Our execution sucks." She smiled at me.

"Do-over?" I held out a hand to Ivy. Yelling and upfront questioning wasn't working. I was going to have to stick to her like glue if I had any hope of figuring out what was going on. And a fresh start was the only way to do that.

"Sure." She fist-bumped my open hand and kept walking. I felt like we'd put a bandage on a cut that kept splitting wider. Popping a piece of Juicy, I tamped down on the sick feeling that bubbled up in my stomach.

We walked the rest of the way to school in silence. I kept replaying the facts of the case as we knew them, trying to figure out what we'd missed. I had no idea what was going on in Ivy's head. She plowed through the slush, her eyebrows drawn together in contemplation.

"Wallace! Mason!" Mr. Williams shouted at us from the corner of the schoolyard. He flailed his arms, beckoning us over.

"So much for keeping things under the radar," I said.

"Updates," Mr. Williams said as we walked up to him. "I want 'em and I want 'em now."

"Well, sir . . .," I started.

"Not here," he hissed. "Honestly, Wallace. A little finesse goes a long way. Come on, come on, come on." Mr. Williams hustled us into the school and down to his office. After checking to make sure the hall was clear, he shut the door and sat behind his desk. "Now, talk."

"We don't have much," I said. "We've eliminated a number of suspects and we're continuing to narrow down the field."

"What are you, a politician?" The coach drummed his hands on the desk and took a slug from his water bottle. "I need details. Facts. Cold, hard evidence. What am I paying you for?"

I bit down on the retort that was struggling to escape from my mouth. "These things take time," I said.

"Much like a mascot," Mr. Williams said. "Time is something we do not *have*." He wiped an arm across his forehead. "I'm going to level with you kids. Things have not been going very well for us this year."

"With the team?" Ivy drew her notebook out of her bag.

"Yes, with the team," the coach said. "We're having our

worst season in twenty years. The guys play like snails. Our bus broke down last month, and I had to pull every string I had in order to get us one for the tri-county tournament. Which we lost. Sparty's gone. The Parents' Association is talking about pressuring the school into appointing a new coach. We need to win this weekend."

"We're working on it," I said.

"Work faster," Mr. Williams said, leaning forward over the desk. "Work like your grades depend on it."

"Are you threatening us?"

"Yes." The coach nodded enthusiastically. "Find me Spartacus, or you fail."

"Glad we cleared that up."

Ivy and I showed ourselves out of the office. Mr. Williams called out after us, "I want that dog by Saturday morning!"

Hurrying up the hall to our lockers, I racked my brain trying to figure out which stone we'd left unturned. "We have to figure this out," I said. "There's got to be something we missed."

"Retrace our steps?" Ivy suggested.

"We checked out the team, checked out Stoverton, checked out Miles," I said. "What else is there?"

"We never finished checking out the team," Ivy said.

“Basketball. Face. Scrambled noggin. Remember?”

“Vividly.” I poked at my still-tender cheek. “We never searched the locker room either. Maybe that’s the key.”

“You’re going to make me miss lunch again, aren’t you?” Ivy sighed.

“When duty calls, you get it to go.”

Chapter Twenty-One

"I'm not investigating on an empty stomach," Ivy said, shutting her locker with a snap. "Any evidence that's been sitting there all week is not going to disappear in the two seconds it'll take me to buy lunch."

My stomach growled before I could answer, and Ivy laughed. "Exactly," she said. "Come on." She hauled me by the arm of my lucky coat, speeding through the doors of the crowded cafeteria. I spotted a familiar face as Ivy zipped over to the relatively short lunch line.

"Hey," I said, sliding into a chair next to Leyla at the bake sale table. "I didn't know you were part of the Arts Council."

She smacked at my wandering fingers, making their way toward a butter tart, and rolled her eyes. "I'm not," she said.

"Ashi roped me into watching the table while she looked for Mrs. Pamuk. Apparently Mr. Williams is trying to kick them out of this spot so the team can sell tickets for Saturday. It's a whole thing."

"That's nice of you."

"Meh," Leyla said. "I've got articles to write up, and she was freaking out. I can work here just as well as anywhere else. Hey!" She pointed at a group of kids walking by. "Buy some cookies. You look like you can spare two bucks."

"Two? Ashi told me four."

"She had you pegged." Leyla chuckled. "Your own fault for not reading the sign. I knew I liked that kid." She stuffed the money she'd collected into a little tin and waved at Ivy as she walked up. "Hey, Ivy. I'm teaching Howard about supply and demand."

"Please don't." Ivy grimaced around her sandwich.

"I know plenty," I said, grabbing a cookie off the table, ignoring Ivy's squawk. "Trust me. Ashi owes me this one."

"Speaking of . . ." Ivy said, "where is Ashi? I thought she was in charge of the table today."

Leyla filled her in on the impending eviction by the basketball team, and Ivy let out a low whistle. "Ellis is going to flip out," she said.

"Incoming." Leyla dipped her chin toward the far end of the cafeteria. Mr. Williams was on his way over to our table.

"We'd better go find Ashi and Mrs. Pamuk before Mr. Williams shuts you guys down." Ivy poked at my shoulder, motioning for me to get out of the chair. "Leyla, can you distract him for a bit?"

"Definitely," Leyla said, a terrifying grin cutting across her face. "I want to ask him a few questions for our upcoming issue." Leaving the situation in her intense hands, Ivy and I quick-marched out of the caf and through the doors.

"Where do you think they'll be?" Ivy did a 360 check of the hallway. Process of elimination meant investigating the most likely spots first. I weighed the odds.

"Let's go to Mrs. Pamuk's classroom," I said, turning left. Ivy and I kept our pace on the fine line between brisk and suspicious. Leyla could only stall for so long. We couldn't afford to waste time being hauled aside by a teacher for questioning.

Rounding the next corner, we spotted our target. Ashi stood in front of Mrs. Pamuk's room, brows drawn together in a frown, green glasses sliding down her nose as her fingers flew over her phone. Message complete, she stuffed her phone into her bag and took off at a jog down the hallway.

My detective senses were tingling. I didn't know if it was the set of her jaw or the fact that she'd hosed me on the cookies, but Ashi was looking pretty shifty. I grabbed Ivy's hand to stop her from calling out.

"Wait," I said. "I want to see where she's going."

"Probably to the cafeteria to deal with the table situation," Ivy said.

"Caf's behind us." I jerked a thumb over my shoulder. "Think she's taking the long, long way around?"

My partner looked back at Ashi's retreating form, an argument dancing on the tip of her tongue.

"There's something I can't put my finger on," I said. "Trust me?"

"Ugh, okay, fine," Ivy said. "But if we're doing this, we'd better get going because she's losing us without even trying."

Matching Ashi's pace, Ivy and I kept a safe distance as she led us through the halls. I held Ivy back at the last corner as our final destination became clear. "I think she's going to the music room."

"Maybe Mrs. Pamuk wasn't in class and she's meeting her here. Or—"

"Ashi." A whispered shout cut off Ivy's theories. We peeked around the corner to see Scotty shuffle running from the other end of the hall toward Ashi. They held a whispered conversation, too low for us to hear, but punctuated by a great deal of arm waving. Ashi shushed Scotty into submission, and he opened up the door to the music room, ushering her inside.

I looked back at my partner. "I think we should—"

"Yes, obviously," she said, pushing me forward. "Go, go."

We tiptoed up to the doors before realizing our predicament. There was no way to get into the room without alerting Scotty and Ashi to our presence. Ivy pointed to the grate at the bottom of the door. In a more shielded environment, it'd be an ideal eavesdropping tool. But out in the hallway, we were totally exposed. Anyone walking by would have at least one question about why we were crouched up against the door. Ivy dropped down, making the decision for us. I followed suit, keeping one ear tuned to the hallway and the other pressed up against the grate.

I was greeted by an explosion of sneezes. "I can't do this anymore," Scotty said, his voice muffled as he struggled to breathe and talk with a head full of snot. "The stress, the hiding, the allergies—it's too much."

"I know, I know," Ashi answered. "It's getting intense. I want to bring him back, but everyone else said no."

"Spartacus?" I mouthed at my partner. Ivy's eyes widened.

"What are they waiting for?" Scotty asked between sneezes.

"They said we have to prove our point, or nothing will change," the girl said. "We'll keep him until after the game on Saturday. Can you handle that?"

"No," Scotty cried. "Look at me. I'm a mess. Listen, I know you can't take him, but there's someone who can. Someone we can trust."

The few beats of silence had me straining closer for Ashi's reply.

"What are you talking about? What did you do, Scotty?" A chair squeaked across the floor. I squinted through the grate, just able to see Ashi's legs pacing around the room. "You can't bring anyone else into this," she said. "We had a pact to keep us all safe."

"He understands," Scotty replied. "He wants to help, and we can't keep passing you-know-who around. We're bound to get caught. No one will ask questions at his house."

"Who is it?"

Scotty's answer was muffled by the scrape of a chair as Ashi sat back down. Her sigh filled the room. "I don't know," she said. "When were you going to make the swap?"

"Today," Scotty said. "You can come by my house after school and check it out. Ask all the questions you want."

Her next words were covered up by a loud, wet, trumpeting blast as Scotty blew his nose. “Thank you,” he said. “I can’t wait to be able to breathe again.”

I was up off the ground the instant their footsteps headed toward the door, Ivy lightning-quick beside me. Running down the hall was a far cry from inconspicuous. We needed a quick escape. I glanced around and, decision made, hauled Ivy along with me. Flying three steps forward, I pushed us through the door across the hall, letting it quietly swing shut behind us.

Ivy stared at the urinals and yellow-tinged floor before taking in the sinks dotted with wads of wet toilet paper. She rolled her eyes at me and I shrugged. Wasn’t my fault that the boys’ bathroom was the closest unlocked room. An emergency escape is never perfect.

“Well,” Ivy said, “I understand why we never hold our meetings in here.”

I waved a hand to shush her as I listened to Scotty and Ashi’s retreat. Scotty and Ashi. My mind was whirling. Turning back to Ivy, I shook my head. “What have they gotten themselves into? What are they thinking? How many people are involved in this?”

“Excellent questions,” Ivy said. “Maybe ones we should pose to Scotty and Ashi?”

"No, no," I said. "We need more information before giving them the opportunity to lie . . . like they have been . . . this whole time." That was going to take a while to sink in.

"You're in Drama Club with Ashi. You haven't heard anything? Noticed anything?"

"Howard, I'm in Drama Club, but I'm not *in* Drama Club." Ivy dismissed my question. "I go to the meetings—"

"Sometimes."

"Unnecessary sass," she said, pausing midpace to cut me some side-eye. "I go to the meetings, but only for fun. I don't get involved in the politics. But Ashi does. She's on the Arts Council too."

We stood in the bathroom, listening to water gurgle in the drain as we processed this new development. Ivy shook her head. "They must have a good reason. They wouldn't do something like this without a real reason."

"Trust me, we're going to find out what it is, but reason or not, now we've got facts. We know who's got Spartacus and where." I grinned. "Now we can steal him back."

"*Steal* him?" Ivy's eyes widened. "How do you figure we'll do that?"

"Luckily," I said. "We know a thief and he owes us a favor."

Chapter Twenty-Two

Scotty lived in an older area of town, full of two-story yellow brick houses and gardens that looked like they didn't dare put a leaf out of place. Each sidewalk lined up precisely with the front door, and every driveway was banished to the rear, off the alleyway. Asphalt had no place in these picture-perfect yards. The Home and Garden Society enforced that rule with an iron fist.

"Which one is Scotty's house?" Ivy asked, looking down the row. I pointed out one in the middle, reconsidered, and slid my hand to point at the one on the right. "Really?"

"Ninety percent sure it's that one," I said. "No, you know what, ninety-five percent sure." Blue had been navigating last time we were here, so I couldn't be faulted for a fuzzy memory. Now that we had our target, it was time to infiltrate. Scoping out the street, I made note of the sole car taking up space three doors over. Our path was clear.

We made our way down the back alley, crouching low to keep our heads below the fence line. I counted off the yards until I realized I'd never checked how many houses in we'd need to go before we started. My partner bumped into me as I stopped short.

"Is this it?"

"Yes," I said, popping my head up to check out the back of the house—looked close enough, anyway.

Ivy took one look at my face and scowled. "You forgot to count, didn't you?"

"I was testing to see if you were counting," I said.

"I can see why you called me," said a voice from the shed behind us. Toby came into view, shaking his head. "You definitely need my help."

"Hey, Toby," Ivy said, grabbing on to my sleeve. "Howard, can we talk for a minute? Over here?" She dragged me back up the alley, out of Toby's hearing. "Why are we using Toby for this? I thought we were supposed to be curbing the criminal element in Grantleyville."

"We need someone with his skill set if we have to break into Scotty's house."

"Break into—we're not breaking into Scotty's house," Ivy hissed.

"If I see Spartacus in there, we are," I said, waving away the rest of her protests. "Ivy, we're so close to cracking this case, I can taste it. We use Toby, we're in, we're out, problem solved."

"I don't like it," she said. "This doesn't feel right."

"You're the one who wanted to stop trading in favors," I said. "I'm clearing them off the books. He owes us for not turning him in, and now we're square. Don't worry about it." I walked back over to Toby. "It's this one here," I said, pointing to the wooden fence.

"Up and over, eh?" He lugged a garbage can around and scrambled on top. Grabbing onto the top of the fence, he hauled himself onto the narrow edge. "You coming?"

Gritting my teeth, I climbed up on the can and took a deep breath. Sweat pooled down my back. Good thing my lucky coat was extra-absorbent.

"Howard," Toby whispered, "what's the holdup?"

"He doesn't like heights," Ivy said from behind me.

Toby leapt nimbly off the fence, making a tidy landing in the snow. "Come on," he said. "It's, like, four feet."

"Not all of us are part spider monkey," I said, hiking myself on top of the fence. I clung on with all four limbs as I tried to gently tilt my body to the other side.

"Today, Howard." Toby tugged on the end of my coat. The sudden pull caught me off guard and I fell the rest of the way, landing in a heap at Toby's feet.

I glared up at him. "That was not helpful."

"Well, it helped you make it over the fence, so I'm going to have to disagree." He held out a hand, and I used it to haul myself up.

Ivy stayed on the other side to keep watch while Toby and I made our way to the back porch. Keeping close to the winter-wrapped foliage, we looked for signs of life in the house. Spartacus was nowhere in sight.

I tried the back door. Locked. "Think you can pick this?"

"Sure." Toby examined the lock and then squinted over my shoulder at a faint rustling sound. "What kind of dog did you say Spartacus was?"

"Pug."

"So, not a gigantic, angry-looking Rottweiler that sleeps

in that dog kennel I thought was a shed and who is now on his way over here with a mouth full of teeth?"

"What—?" A low growl cut me off. Out of the corner of my eye, I spotted a dark brown muzzle nosing toward the pocket of my lucky coat.

"Howard!" Ivy's head popped up over the back fence. "What's going on?"

"Bit of a situation here," I said through clenched teeth.

"What's in your pocket?" Toby asked.

"Pack o' Juicy."

"Toss it to him," Toby said.

"You can't give gum to a dog," Ivy hollered. The three of us turned to look at her, arms hanging over the side of the fence. She must have been standing on her tiptoes on the garbage can. "It's poisonous."

"Well, it's give the dog the gum or let him chew on me," I said. Ivy remained quiet while the beast continued to snuffle at my coat, a light growl humming in his throat. "Any ideas at this point are welcome."

"I got it!" Ivy snapped her fingers and disappeared.

"Good dog," Toby said, receiving a sidelong glare and a full growl for his efforts.

"Toby?"

"Yup?"

"Don't talk."

A rattling crash signaled the return of Ivy. "Okay," she said. "I've got half a date bar from lunch. I'll call Mr. Pups and you guys go over the side fence to the next yard."

"Mr. P—you named it?"

"I'm creating a bond so he'll listen to me. Don't question my lifesaving methods, Howard Wallace!"

I was gonna die.

"Okay, fine. Do it." I looked at Toby. "Wait until he's far enough away and then book it."

Ivy flourished the date bar over the fence. "Here, Mr. Pups! Good boy! Puppy want a snack? Yes, you do! Yes, you do-o!"

Mr. Pups, the hellhound, barked and loped over to Ivy. When he reached the far end of the yard, I shoved Toby, and we started running. Mr. Pups, sensing that all was not right, skidded to a stop in front of Ivy. His eyes darted between us and the treat. Toby reached the fence and started hauling himself up over the top. With unexpected grace, Mr. Pups leapt up and snatched the date bar out of Ivy's hand. She shrieked, caught off guard by the sudden move, and toppled backward off the trash can.

Triumph oozing from every pore, the beast tossed the bar in the air and swallowed it in one gulp. His snarls and barks heralded my impending doom. Ropelike strips of saliva flicked through the air as he began his charge.

"Give me your hand!" Fingers flapped in front of my face, and I looked up to see Toby sitting on the fence. I grabbed hold and he pulled with all his might until I was flopped over the fence, legs flapping in the wind. "Here he comes!" Toby shouted. He threw himself into the other yard, taking me with him. The fence shuddered as Mr. Pups slammed against it, but luckily it held. I lay on the ground, waiting for my heart to find its way back into my chest.

"Thanks, man," I said, glancing over at Toby, who was also enjoying a moment of supine recuperation.

"No problem."

Groaning as I sat up, I shook my head. We still didn't have what we came for. I was not going to let this case get the best of me. A small whimper came from my left.

"Was that you?" I turned to Toby.

"No," he said, flipping onto his stomach. "You said we're looking for a pug, right?"

I followed his gaze and spotted Spartacus standing a few feet away, watching us with his odd little bug eyes. One house over the whole time. Only took a near-mauling to find him.

Our discovery was interrupted by the slow screeching of Ivy dragging her trash can over to the next fence. Three bangs and a crash later, her head came into view. "You alive?"

"Yeah. And look who we found."

"Oh, he's cute. OK. Are we done with this ridiculousness?"

"Yes." Toby got himself upright and scooped up Spartacus. "Let's go."

"Hang on," I said, brushing myself off as I stood. "We should try and gather some evidence."

"First rule of crime, Howard Wallace," he said. "When you get your goods, get gone."

Spartacus chose that moment to let out a wild flurry of barks. The back door of the house opened and Scotty stood there with Ashi, looking more confused than usual. "Spartacus, what's wrong bo—Howard?"

"See?" Toby shoved Spartacus into my arms. "Consider us even now." He sprinted to the back fence and flipped over it without a moment's hesitation.

"'Bye, Toby," Ivy called out from her perch. "Make good choices."

"Howard?" Scotty stepped forward. "What are you doing?"

"My job," I said, backing slowly away toward my partner.

Ashi held up her hands, shaking her head. "You can't. You don't understand."

"I understand that this dog isn't yours and you're causing a lot of people some serious grief."

"They started it," she said. "We're doing what needs to be done. Ivy, let us explain."

I passed Spartacus up to Ivy. She patted him as he licked at her chin and wriggled in her arms. "Look," she said, resting her elbow on the fence, "we know that you guys didn't do this for kicks, and we want to hear you out."

Scotty and Ashi took a step off the back porch, shoulders drooping in relief.

"But we have a duty to our clients," I said. "We need to get Spartacus back to his owner."

"No, you can't," Ashi cried out.

"I like you guys plenty, but you've been lying to us this whole time." I adjusted my lucky coat, taking a minute to collect my thoughts. "We need to take care of our business first. Spartacus can be returned without involving you, and then we can help you out of whatever mess you're in."

"Howard, please wait." Scotty's voice went up a notch, and the back door opened again.

"Are you guys coming back in with Sparty? I need to get home soon."

Ivy's sharp intake of breath and my ears told me what I still needed to see with my own eyes. I looked up at the porch. Miles Fletcher, in the flesh, pulling the door shut behind him.

"Oh," he said. "Hi."

"Hi? *Hi?*" I scoffed. "We catch you in the middle of a criminal act, and you say 'hi'?"

Miles joined Scotty and Ashi at edge of the yard. "Criminal act? Howard, come on."

"Aiding and abetting a pugnapping, obstructing an investigation, evidence tampering." I listed off the points. "Want me to continue?"

"No," Miles said. "I want you to listen."

"Yeah, he's helping us," Scotty said, running a hand over his miserable nose.

"He's helping you? Ivy, I changed my mind. We're going to hear them out now."

"Hey," she murmured to me. I looked back to see her tucking a shivering Spartacus inside her coat. "I think coming back later might be a better idea."

"No, no, no," I said, spinning back to Miles and his gang.

"I want to hear all of the great reasons you guys have for destroying someone's reputation and leading us on a wild goose chase."

"Miles only got involved today," Scotty said. "He caught me in the middle of an allergy attack and figured out that I had Spartacus. I was too tired to lie about it. His hair gets everywhere. I can't sleep with all of this sneezing."

The fact that Miles had put those clues together only added to the insult burning in my gut. "I'm a little confused," I said, facing him. "You're helping Scotty and Ashi with what, exactly?"

"Hiding Spartacus," Ashi supplied. "Our parents were getting suspicious."

"And this was going to be before or after you helped us find Spartacus and brought his abductors to Mr. Williams to clear your good friend Carl?"

Scotty and Ashi began to shift on their feet, shooting Miles some nervous side-eye as he stayed silent.

"Which one is it? Are you helping us or helping them? Or are they both lies?" I said, stepping nose to nose with Miles. "And you're still just helping yourself?"

"I was trying to fix it," he burst out. "I was trying to help you and Carl and when I found out Scotty was involved, I thought I could help him, too."

"Stop *lying*." I took a deep breath and forced myself to lower my voice. A broken laugh escaped instead. "I am sick and tired of people lying to me."

"You're in the wrong line of work then," Miles muttered.

I lost the volume control battle. "You think this is the time for jokes?"

"Howard," Ivy called from the fence. "I think we should go."

Miles reached out and gripped my sleeve. "How do I convince you I'm not lying?"

"You let us leave," I said, shaking my arm loose. "Let us work on cleaning up this mess. All three of you."

"But—" Ashi shot a stricken look at Spartacus, and Scotty put a hand on her shoulder.

"Let him go, Ashi. Howard can make it right."

I spun on my heel and strode toward the fence. Ivy hopped off the can, making room for me as I flopped over. We walked down the alley, and no one made a move to follow. I couldn't get the three faces out of my mind. Ashi, blinking with fear, Scotty, full of trust, and Miles, resigned to his fate. This case had gotten three times messier in the span of one break-in.

"Howard . . ." Ivy began, and I shook my head.

“Not now,” I said. “We deal with it at the office.”

Ivy nodded as our feet slid down icy sidewalks. Spartacus sighed from his spot inside her coat. We’d found our man—well, *dog*. But somehow, it didn’t feel like a victory.

Chapter Twenty-Three

We arrived back at the garage office and hustled Spartacus inside. Free from Ivy's arms, he immediately started nosing around. His wet snuffling filled the silence.

"How are you going to explain this to your folks?" Ivy leaned up against the desk.

"Spartacus?" I watched as he drooled enthusiastically on Blue's rear tire. She managed to stay calm, but I could tell her composure was slipping. "I'll tell them we found him on our walk," I said, scooping up Spartacus and plopping him on the comfy, stinky chair. "They don't need all the details—just that we found him and we're returning him to the coach tomorrow."

"Then what? What's the plan here, Howard?"

"What it's always been. We get Spartacus back to Mr. Williams, clear Carl, and get ourselves free of this whole mess."

"How exactly does that clear Carl?" Ivy propelled away from the desk, sliding it a few inches with the force of her movement.

"The only evidence Mr. Williams has against Carl is a lack of Spartacus." I poked my desk back into place. "He can't accuse him of dognapping when the dog's right in front of him."

"He's going to want to know what happened, Howard. He thinks Carl's involved. We can't just say 'here's your dog' and call it a day."

"Why not?" It was the most appealing of all our options, as traveling back in time and not taking the case in the first place wasn't in the cards.

Ivy leveled a look at me. "I seriously have to spell this out for you? He can still keep Carl off the team for losing Spartacus. We have to prove it was done deliberately by someone else."

Irritation burned in my gut even though I knew Ivy was right—one snag on the heels of a hundred others. Frustration bloomed as my patience hit its breaking point, and I sank into the desk chair, rubbing at my forehead.

Our options were limited. Clients had to come first. "So we give him Ashi and Scotty," I finally said.

"Howard!" Ivy's mouth fell open and Spartacus growled softly.

"What? You said we have to expose who's responsible. Well, we know who did it—the people who've been lying to us all week. Lying and sending us on wild-goose chases. Are you saying we should protect them over Carl?"

"I don't even know what to say to that." My partner paced in front of the desk. "Okay, yes I do. Two things. First of all, they're our friends."

I raised an eyebrow, and Ivy fluttered a hand in the air. "They're people we're friendly with," she said. "More importantly, they're two of the least criminally minded individuals we know. How are your detective senses not tingling? They stole a dog and covered it up. Don't you want to know why?"

"Obviously, we don't know them as well as we thought we did," I said. "And of course, I want to know why. It's been hounding me all the way home. But I wasn't about to turn around and—"

Ivy's face softened as she realized where the end of that sentence was going. I wasn't about to turn around after that blowup with Miles.

Miles, who kept popping up in every corner of this case. Ruining the one space that was mine.

"Maybe you should talk to him," Ivy said softly.

"That's the last thing I need," I said, pulling a pad of paper out of the top drawer. "He shouldn't have been involved in the first place. Miles is out of the equation."

"Howard . . ." Ivy's laugh held a bitter edge. "Miles *is* the equation. You've been trying to rush this case along since you saw him in Carl's driveway. Now you're cutting corners so you don't have to deal with him anymore." She put a hand over the papers on the desk, forcing me to look up at her. "But case or no case, you're always going to have to deal with him. Why are you punishing Scotty and Ashi for that?"

"They stole a dog, Ivy. Punishment kind of comes with that package."

She shook her head. "You're not listening to me."

"I'm listening just fine," I said. "Yeah, I'm mad at Miles. And Scotty. And Ashi. I don't like it when people lie and betray me. It's a flaw, I know."

Ivy pointed a finger in my direction. "Don't get snippy," she said.

"Hard not to when you're accusing me of cutting corners." I hauled myself out of the chair and yanked Carl's file out of the cabinet. "Which is pretty rich coming from someone who's missed half the case," I said, slamming the drawer shut. "Are you only interested when it's convenient for you?"

"That's not fair," Ivy drew in a shaky breath. "You don't know—"

"I know we have one day until the Grudge Game," I cut her off. "We don't have the time to mess around."

Spartacus whined, and Ivy dropped down beside him to stroke his head. "I didn't think a thorough investigation was 'messing around.' "

"I'm not talking about this with you anymore." I grabbed my hat off the desk and shoved it onto my head. "Helping Ashi and Scotty is not our job. Our job is done. I'm in charge, and I say—"

Ivy jerked back. "You're in charge?" She narrowed her eyes at me. "What—am I only your partner if I agree with you?"

"No. *No.* That's not what I meant." I scrubbed a hand over my face, realizing what I'd said. This conversation had gone completely off the rails. "It's been a really long day, and I think we need a break. I'm going to go get Spartacus some water and I'll get us some snacks."

I walked out of the garage and into the house. Searching through the kitchen cupboards for a suitable bowl, I let out a frustrated breath. It wasn't as if Ivy and I had never fought. We argued all the time. But this felt different. The crack was running deep, and I didn't know how to fix it. I randomly picked up a bowl and stuck it under the faucet. I knew I should go apologize for yelling. I could do that. Apologize and get things back on track. Easy.

Heading out to the garage, water-filled bowl in hand, I tucked a bag of pretzels under my other arm. "Look, Ivy—" I froze in the doorway, taking in the empty room.

Ivy was gone.

And she'd taken Spartacus with her.

Chapter Twenty-Four

My own partner had just pooched our case. I ran out to the driveway, water sloshing over the sides of the bowl. "Ivy!" The streetlights were popping on one by one, illuminating a distinct lack of Ivy in the area. She and Spartacus must have been hoofing it to make it off our street so quickly. "Ivy!" Ineffective as it was, yelling provided slight relief to my predicament.

I hurled the water out onto the lawn on my way back into the garage. We never should have taken this case. It'd started out hinky and gone downhill from there. Now, with Ivy gone rogue, taking Spartacus with her, I was left with nothing to offer Carl and Marvin but a shoddy excuse for poor workmanship.

Cursing, I slammed a hand down on the desk. Blue creaked in her corner, and I sighed. “Language, yourself,” I said. Ignoring the baleful stare of her headlight, I sunk into my chair. Serious thinking was required.

First step was to get Spartacus back. *Again.*

No.

First step was to ask my partner what on earth she was thinking. Then get Spartacus back. Then get him to the coach. Then clear Carl’s name and be rid of this case.

A folded piece of paper on the desk caught my eye. I flipped it open to find Ivy’s fierce print scrawled across the page.

This is the right thing to do. Trust me.

Trust her. How was I supposed to trust the person going behind my back?

I crumpled up the note and tossed it on the floor. “I’ll clean it up later,” I hollered at Blue on my way out the door. Striding up to the house, I kicked at piles of snow as I went. The door slammed behind me, and Pops stuck his head around the corner from the hallway. “Hey, bud, what did that door do to you?”

Mumbling an apology, I yanked off my coat and tossed it over a hook. I grabbed the house phone from the kitchen and punched in Ivy's number. No answer. A second try took me straight to voicemail. Trying not to tip off Pops, I whisper-yelled a message into the phone. "I know you think you know what you're doing, Ivy, but you don't know, and what you're doing is ruining our case." I paused for a breath. "Call me back."

"Howard," Pops said, coming up behind me, dropping a hand on my shoulder, "let's talk." He steered me toward the kitchen table and plunked me in a chair. He pulled one up in front of me. Hands on his knees, he leaned forward. "You first."

The man had terrible timing. I was in the middle of a crisis and he wanted to shoot the breeze. "What are we talking about, Pops?"

"What's going on with you, for starters," he said, crossing a leg and getting way too comfortable for my liking. "Sounds like you and Ivy are having a spot of trouble."

"We're having a difference of opinion," I said. "We're working on a—" I remembered the no-working-cases-during-the-week rule right on time. "Working on a project and we're having a difference of opinion. She won't listen. And now, she seems to think sabotaging it is the better plan."

Pops nodded. "And by project, you mean case."

I stumbled over a response and he swatted away my protests. "I'm not an idiot, Howard. And you're not as subtle as you think."

"How long have you known?"

"Since you and Ivy came home on Sunday and locked yourselves in the garage office. What's happening?"

I filled him in on everything, starting with Marvin calling in his favor, through Coach's involvement, the Miles factor, Ivy's weird behavior, and ending with her very recent betrayal. He sat back and digested it all. "I think," he said, finally, "you've forgotten about rule number two."

Unlikely. They were etched into my detective DNA. "Ask the right questions," I replied.

"Your problem isn't the case; it's with Ivy. You guys aren't working together like you should. You've been asking where she is and what she's doing, but not why. Not why would she take Spartacus, but why is she so upset?"

This was the last thing I needed right now. "Or," I said, sitting up in my chair, "why is my partner acting like a lunatic and destroying our reputations?"

Pops leveled a look at me. "It sounds like Ivy has a lot going on. I think she could use a friend, not a partner."

"We're supposed to be both," I muttered.

"Exactly," Pops said. "Maybe another good question to ask yourself is why you've been neither."

I flinched. "Whose side are you on?"

"Ivy's," he said. "One hundred percent."

"Thanks, Pops."

"Listen, Howard," he said, propping an elbow up on the table. "There comes a time in every friendship where you hit a rocky patch and either you forge ahead or you fall apart." He waited a beat until I looked up and made eye contact. "Do you want things with Ivy to fall apart?"

If the current state of things was anything to judge by, they already were. "But I don't know what to do."

"You have to learn to see outside your own bubble," he continued. "You have a partnership. It's not solely about what you feel and what you want anymore. If you want to fix things, you have to go talk to her."

"I was planning on doing that, anyway."

"Not about Spartacus." Pops shook his head. "Ivy's your case now. Figure out what you missed."

Chapter Twenty-Five

The next morning, the sky decided to join me in my wretched mood. The dark, gray clouds dripped a freezing mix of snow and rain, which covered Grantleyville in a clumpy coat of misery. Pops dropped me off at school barely on time.

I skirted through the trails of slush in the hallway, chucked my stuff in my locker, and made it into my homeroom class just as the bell rang. Ms. Kowalski looked up, raising an eyebrow. "Skin of your teeth, Howard Wallace," she tutted. "Skin of your teeth."

Sliding into my chair, I took a gander back at Ivy's seat. Empty. Ms. Kowalski took attendance, skipping over my partner's name. I flung my hand into the air, straining forward as Ms. Kowalski studiously ignored me. She continued down the list, her eyes never leaving the paper. I spread my fingers out as far as they would go to make a bigger visual target. A muscle began to twitch in her cheek. After the last answer of "Here" she slowly lowered the page and stared at me. A loud squeak cut through the classroom chatter as I inched forward in my chair.

"Yes, Howard?" She bit each word off, grinding the last syllable to dust.

"Where's Ivy?"

"You don't know the whereabouts of your own partner-in-crime?"

"I'd say it's partner-in-crime-*solving* at least ninety percent of the time, but we can argue about that later. Where is she? Is she sick?"

"The office marked her absent, so your guess is as good as mine," she said. "If I may continue with our day?"

I nodded, lost in thought. It wasn't like Ivy to miss school. Although, she also usually wasn't trying to conceal evidence of thievery. I'd have to swing by her place after school and knock on the door until she answered.

-. .. -.-. -.-   .- -. -..   -. --- .-. .-

When lunchtime rolled around, I followed the flow of traffic to the cafeteria. It felt weird going by myself. I'd gotten used to having Ivy around to talk my ear off. Maybe I'd go eat with Pete. Before I could ponder tracking him down, an arm whipped out of a doorway and hauled me by the collar into an empty classroom. I caught myself on a desk before I could topple over. Straightening up, I came face to face with the last person I expected to be hauling me around by the collar.

"Scotty."

"Howard," he smiled sheepishly.

"What's going on?"

He nodded over my shoulder, and I spun around. Nearly a dozen seats were filled with vaguely familiar kids. Ashi waved from the front row. Standing by the window was an imposing figure, backlit by the faded winter sun.

"Welcome, Howard," the figure said, pushing away from the sill and walking toward me. Black hair framed a narrow face that watched me with calculating eyes. "Glad you could make it."

"What have I made?" I took in the scene and adjusted my rumpled coat. "Secret society? Howard Wallace Appreciation Club? Is there punch and pie?"

"I heard you were funny." She came to stand next to me, wiping a speck of lint from my collar. "I suppose rumors do get blown out of proportion."

The room and the face had been my first clue, but the theatrics clinched it. "Ellis Garcia," I said, holding out a hand. "Nice to finally have the pleasure. What does the head of the Arts Council, and I'm guessing the rest of the council, want with me?"

She gave my hand a solid shake and smiled.

"A détente, if you will," she said, spreading her hands out wide. "We're hoping the opportunity to hear our side will make things progress a little more . . . reasonably."

"I prefer not to be manhandled into negotiations," I said.

"My apologies for that," Ellis said. "We didn't think you'd come for a chat willingly."

Pops's words wound their way back through my brain. Ivy wanted to hear them out, so I'd hear them out. "I'm listening," I said.

Ellis gestured to the nearest table, and we sat. Everyone else scooched their chairs in closer. "This is the GMS Arts Council," Ellis said. "We represent all the clubs from Drama to Writers' Workshop. Banding together was the best bet to make ourselves heard."

"Not that it worked," someone griped.

"The goal is to get more support for our programs," Ellis continued.

I sat back in my chair. "What does this have to do with Spartacus?"

"I'm getting to that," she said. "Since the beginning of the year, our already pitiful budget has been slashed and redirected to the basketball team."

The other kids chimed in all at once.

"They took half of our spring musical money to put toward the new scoreboard."

"They needed a bus for an away game, so they bumped our field trip."

"We still haven't rescheduled."

"All of our fund-raisers get booted out of the gym for games and practices."

Ellis stood up, slamming a hand down on the desk. "We get shoved to the side again and again, and no one cares. Mrs. Pamuk tried to help, but she's no match for the Parents' Association. They only want sports and more sports." She sat back down in her chair. "Desperate times call for desperate measures," she said. "If we didn't do something to get people to take notice, all of our programs were going to fold."

The "why" was starting to make a lot more sense. Except . . .

"How did Scotty get roped into all of this?"

"I'm in band," Scotty said. "Oboes before b-balls, Howard."

"Of course," I said. "I should have realized."

"Except I play trumpet, but there's no good sports rhyme for that. But you know what I mean—"

"Scotty, I get it." Clearer motivation didn't make this any less of a mess. "What was your plan outside of kidnapping Spartacus? Were you really willing to let Carl take the fall for everything?"

"We wanted to let the basketball team fail," Ellis said. "Let them get a taste of being second-class citizens. We'd figure out a way to get Carl cleared before it went too far."

"Getting kicked off the basketball team and threatened with suspension is pretty far," I said.

"I said we were working on it," Ellis muttered.

Despite their ever-so-slightly higher moral ground, the Art Council's bad methodology was burying them up to their necks in repercussions. Someone needed to take charge.

"Okay," I said. "Here's what we're going to do." I laid out a plan on the fly—a last-ditch effort to clear Carl, help the team, and keep the Arts Council kids out of a lifetime of detention.

Ellis shook her head. "That's a terrible plan."

"Happens to be my speciality, sweetheart," I said. "Besides, it's better than what you've got."

"Don't call me sweetheart." She paused and gave me a piercing look. "You're really going to help?"

"Gonna try." I stood up and nodded to the group. "I'll be in touch."

I made my way out of the room and into the hall. Pulling a notebook out of my pocket, I jotted down some ideas for how to proceed. I wanted to make sure I had everything set when I talked to Ivy. Movement to my left caught my eye. Quick as lightning, the door to the girls' bathroom opened and a hand snaked out, hauling me inside. I grabbed onto the sink to prevent a face plant.

"Whatever happened to a nice 'Howard, may I speak to you?' Everyone's all hands today." Righting myself, I came face to face with Carl and Leyla. Disconcerting on many fronts.

I shot a look at Leyla. "How many of my offices are you going to steal?"

"Haven't decided," she mused. "Might check out your home digs and make it a hat trick."

Not sure if that was a sports reference or a dig at my wardrobe. Either way I was annoyed. "It's always a slice with you two, but in case you've forgotten, I'm working a case. I don't have time for shenanigans."

"That's what we want to talk to you about," Leyla said. "I thought you were bringing Spartacus to school today?"

I cursed our info-sharing agreement and the random fit of cooperation that had me filling her in before we left for Scotty's place yesterday. "About that," I said. "Change of plans. Ivy's got Spartacus right now, and we're working on a plan to bring him back to the school."

"Why do you need a plan? You bring him back. Boom, done," Leyla said. Carl nodded.

Checking the stalls quickly for interlopers, I bought myself some time to come up with something reasonable. A tiny voice that sounded suspiciously like Ivy's piped up in my head. *You know what's reasonable? The truth.*

"That's rarely the case," I murmured.

"Tick tock, Howard," Leyla said. "I've got a deadline to meet, Carl's got a game to play, and I assume you'd like to solve this case, but I'm not putting any money on that one."

I did want to solve this case, but it was proving easier said than done. Especially without my partner.

Carl was watching me with a steady gaze as Leyla continued her lecture on follow-through. "What'd you do?" he asked, cutting off the barrage.

"Excuse me?"

"No Spartacus, no Ivy," he said. "Kind of suspicious you're the one left standing."

Why was it that whenever Carl chose to speak, it was to make things more inconvenient for me? "Here's my question for you guys," I said. "Do you trust me?"

"No," Carl said.

"Not even a little bit," Leyla added.

Wrong tack.

"Okay, Leyla. Do you want the biggest story this school has ever had?"

Her eyes lit up. "More than anything."

"Carl, do you want to return to the basketball team, not merely as a player, but as a hero?"

"No, I just want to play."

"Two out of three ain't bad." I held up a hand before they could ask. "I'm counting myself because I need the boost and obviously I agree with my own plan."

"Which. Is. What?" Leyla tapped out an impatient tattoo on the sink.

"I need more time. I'm going to talk to Ivy after school, and then I'll meet you guys at Marvin's. Six o'clock?"

"If you're not there," Leyla said, "I'm leading with 'BUMBLING PI LOSES BELOVED MASCOT' for our weekend edition."

"Noted."

We staggered our exits, and I took stock.

Plan. Right.

I had a plan. It stretched the limits of rule number six, but it was a plan. If Carl and Leyla stuck with me, I had the muscle and the media. Now I needed an inside man.

Chapter Twenty-Six

The basketball team was having an eleventh-hour practice after school to prep for tomorrow's game. I snuck in a side door and hunkered down by the bleachers. Watching them run laps, I waited for my opportunity. On lap seven, I made a move. Leaning out as far as I could, I grabbed Miles's arm as he ran by and hauled him under the bleachers.

"Howard! What the heck?"

"It's a thing today," I said, getting myself resituated. "Go with it."

"Whatever." He sighed and turned to leave.

"Wait." I held out a hand. "I want to talk to you."

Miles studied me for a long moment, the thump of the team's feet hitting the floor keeping time as the minute stretched out. "Okay," he said finally, taking a seat on the floor beside me. "But we need to be quick. Coach'll notice eventually."

Picking at my sleeve, I rummaged through my thoughts. I'd had all afternoon to prepare and I still didn't know where to start.

"Howard?" Miles prodded.

"I want you to tell me why," I said.

"I told you." He played with his laces, avoiding my scrutiny. "Carl's my friend, and I wanted to help him. And I like Scotty. When I figured out he was involved, I thought I could help him, too." He huffed out a breath. "Not that I did. Definitely made things worse."

I wasn't about to argue that point.

Miles took a quick peek over his shoulder at the team still running through their warm-ups. A tiny smile twitched his lips. "And it was fun," he said. "I always thought you and Ivy were just running around like dorks, but being a P.I. is awesome."

Nobody could fault him for falling under the spell of investigation. Putting together clues and chasing down perps was a top-tier extracurricular activity.

Miles leaned back against the bleachers. "I shouldn't

have gone to Scotty's," he said. "I thought I could take care of it without dealing with you. Seemed easier."

"Fair enough," I said, feeling the truth behind the words. A good chunk of this case had spiraled because of my own desire to not deal with Miles. Time to put an end to that.

"Okay." He eyed me warily. "Was that it?"

"No," I said, taking a deep breath. "That actually wasn't the *why* I meant." Pops had reminded me to ask the right questions. It was time to ask the one I'd been sitting on since last year.

"Why'd you stop being my friend?"

Miles stiffened, staring at the floor. His forehead creased as a frown worked its way down his face. I waited, wondering if this was a question I'd ever have the answer to.

"When I—" Miles coughed and started again. "When I joined the team," he said. "It was like I had the chance to be a new person."

"What was wrong with the old you?"

"You know what it was like," Miles said. I rolled my eyes. Of course I did. Nothing had changed for me. Except now I had Ivy. *Had.*

"I was tired of getting ragged on," he continued. "All of a sudden, I was one of them. We were literally on the same team. Everyone joked around, and we had fun." Miles rubbed a hand over his head. "And when the jokes were about you, I panicked. I remembered what it was like and I thought—" He trailed off.

"Just say it," I whispered.

"A part of me thought it was better you than me," Miles said.

I nodded, not trusting myself to speak. Knowing something was different from hearing it said out loud.

"By that point," Miles said. "You were on my case and being snotty about me joining the team, so another part of me felt like it was payback."

"I was mad," I said. "Of course I was on your case. You ditched me. For *sports*. All of a sudden basketball was the most important thing ever. More important than your best friend."

"It wasn't more important." Miles sighed. "It was just different. People actually talked to me. They noticed me—in a good way. I liked it, even though it was making you hate me." He scratched at his sneaker. "After a while, being mad was easier than thinking about how messed up everything was."

Having a year's worth of mad under my own belt, I understood where he was coming from. I didn't like it, but I understood it. There was one serious point that needed correcting though. "I never hated you," I said, and Miles's head whipped up. "I was mad and upset, but I never hated you."

"I never hated you either," Miles said, swallowing hard.

We sat in silence until the whump of bouncing basketballs filled the gym.

"So," I said, clearing my throat, "do you still want to help?"

"Can I?" Miles's eyebrows quirked at that. "I mean, yeah, if you'll let me."

I explained our current predicament and my makeshift plan.

"First of all, that's a terrible plan," he said. "Second, where do I fit in?"

"I need you to get as many guys from the team on board as possible," I said, laying it out fast before he had a chance to overthink. "They're not going to listen to Scotty, not once they find out he was involved. But we need the numbers to make this work—to make an impression. And the guys will listen to one of their own."

"And if it doesn't work?"

No point in lying. "You could get booted off the team," I said. "Make yourself a target again."

I waited for him to take a pass. Instead, he tilted his head and asked, "Who's on board?"

"Me, obviously," I said, and Miles snorted. "Carl, Leyla, Ashi, Scotty, Ellis, and the rest of the Arts Council."

"Ivy?"

"Yes." Probably.

Hopefully.

"Okay." He nodded. "I'm in."

"Meet me at Marvin's at six," I said, pouncing before he could take it back.

Miles ducked his head and scrambled out from under the bleachers. He stayed crouched, looking over at me. "Hey, Howard?"

"Yeah?"

"Thanks for asking me," he said. "I appreciate it. Even if we end up regretting it."

He jogged back out onto the court, and I waited a beat before crawling out myself. I knew a thing or two about regrets. Collecting them was easy. Clearing them up, not so much. But Pops was right. Sometimes you just had to forge ahead.

It was time to go get my partner back.

Chapter Twenty-Seven

Ivy's house was smack in the middle between my neighborhood and Scotty's. It was two-story red brick with a bare maple tree in the side yard. The grey slush and dirty snow carpeting the yard made for a less-than-inviting picture. I strode up to the front door before I could talk myself out of it and gave three solid knocks. Ivy's grandma came to the door. The temperature took a sudden drop, but I soldiered on.

"Hi, Lillian."

"Howard, please, call me Mrs. Mason."

Ouch. Guess I knew where I stood now. "May I speak to Ivy, please? Ma'am?"

"Sorry," she said, already closing the door. "She's not home."

"I'll wait for her." Desperation moved me forward, and I stuck a foot in the doorway.

Lillian—Mrs. Mason—gave it a pointed look and shot one at my face for good measure. "That's not a good idea, Howard."

"I'm afraid I have to insist."

"I'll tell her you stopped by," Mrs. Mason said, giving my foot a little kick and knocking it off the jamb. "She'll call you."

The door slammed shut, and I stumbled back on the stoop. Less than a success, but not quite a failure. Ivy was definitely at home. My dismissal wouldn't have been so swift if she wasn't. Wandering back to the walkway, I looked up at her window.

There it was.

A twitch in the curtains.

Ivy was watching. Now I had to get her attention. I marched into the yard and checked out my options. There was really only one. I placed a hand on the trunk of the tree and gathered my strength. Onward and upward. After a few false starts, I got a hold and made my way up the tree. The slippery bark almost got the best of me, but I pressed on. I crawled out onto the branch closest to Ivy's window.

"Poor planning, Howard," I muttered. I had nothing to

throw at her window to get her attention. Time for a little classic rule number one. "Ivy," I hollered. "I-vy!"

The window slid open and her face appeared. "What is *wrong* with you?"

"We need to talk," I said, maintaining my death grip on the branch.

"You mean you need to talk," Ivy said. The window skated shut.

"Ivy?"

This was going even less to plan than expected.

"*Ivy.*"

After what felt like another lifetime, the window opened one excruciating inch at a time. My partner reappeared in the window. "What?"

I held her gaze for as long as I could muster, finally managing to get the words out. "I'm stuck."

She closed her eyes and took a deep breath. The glare she came back with would have taken out any poor sap, but I was too preoccupied with my current predicament for any lasting effects. She exhaled in a huff. The window slid back down and Ivy vanished.

"Hello?" I called out. "I don't need much help. A rope would be good. Ladder. Fire department."

The front door slammed and Ivy came into view. Pulling mittens on, she watched me cling to my post and shook her head. My partner grabbed hold of the tree and climbed up to my branch. After getting herself situated while I held on for dear life, she turned to me. "You're an idiot."

"You're right," I said. "And not just about this particular situation. I've been an idiot. I've been a bad partner and a bad friend."

Wind whipped through the tree, and a pile of dead, wet leaves slipped from the branch above onto my head. "Oh, gross." Ivy broke a small smile as I stuck a finger under my collar to dig out the icy cluster. "I've messed up a lot this week," I said. "But the worst mistake I made was messing up with you."

She stayed silent.

"I can keep talking and I'll keep apologizing for as long as it takes. But I really came to see if maybe you wanted to talk about what's been going on with you."

Ivy's eyes welled up. "A lot of stuff, Howard. A lot of stuff."

Shuffling over, I moved in to give her a hug. I felt the exact moment my weight shifted in the wrong direction. Instantly, I released my hold. No point in taking my partner down with me. I caught sight of Ivy's horrified face as I slipped off the branch and fell to the ground.

"Howard!"

"It's okay," I wheezed. "The snow broke my fall."

Ivy clambered down the tree and leaned over me. "Well, at least you're not stuck anymore." She held out a hand and helped me up. "Let's go inside."

-. .. -.-. -.- .- -. -.. -. --- .-. .-

With my lucky coat safely in the dryer, I sat in Ivy's room with a towel around my neck. Ivy was wearing a groove in the floor in front of me, and Spartacus watched the whole scene from his perch on her bed, eyes slightly crossed.

"I don't even know if I want to talk," Ivy said. "I've been talking—to my grandma, my dad—although that's been as much yelling as talking. Talking to my therapist has been good. That's why I skipped out on Drama Club, by the way. She shot me a sideways look. "But she wasn't happy when I missed my Wednesday appointment."

"Why didn't you tell me that's where you were going?"

"When should I have told you? When you were accusing me of taking on other jobs, or when you were peeved at me for not helping with the case enough?"

The full scope of how much I'd messed up began to sink in. Everything I'd missed and ignored. The words knotted up in my throat. "Ivy, I—"

She stopped suddenly to face me. "I'm not going to apologize for taking Spartacus."

"I'm not asking you to," I said with a forceful shake of my head. "You were right."

Ivy blinked. "Yes," she said, nodding. "I was." She stared off at the wall for a moment and then nodded again. Reaching into her bag, she pulled out a wrinkled, white envelope. Her name was scrawled across the front.

"Ivy," I said. "Whatever it is, you don't have to—"

"No." She handed me the envelope. "I want to."

I carefully opened up the envelope and pulled out the paper from inside. It was a single sheet, crumpled, ripped, and taped back together. I skimmed over the contents and blinked. "It's from your mom."

"Yup," Ivy said, snapping off the end of the word with a pop.

"I don't have to read this."

She took the letter out of my hand and folded it back up. "I'll give you the highlights," she said. "She needs time, she has to work on herself, she's not getting back to together with Dad, but she misses me." Ivy's fingers twitched, ripping the edge of the paper. "That keeps happening," she said, reaching for the tape on her desk. "Long story short, she's moving to Grantleyville. Dad's already talking about the schedule for my living arrangements."

"When did she send that?"

"Monday," Ivy said, taping the letter back together and tucking it away. "It came in a packet of divorce papers for my dad. They're talking like it's already done and sorted. Nobody's asking what I want. I'm supposed to fall in line."

"Ivy," I said, sitting forward in my seat. "I'm so sorry."

She waved me off, eyes bright. "It's okay. I mean, it's not okay. Obviously. But it will be. Eventually. It has to be, right?"

"I had no idea."

"Trust me, I know," Ivy said, shooting me a look. She sat down on the bed beside Spartacus. "Listen, I know I punked out on the case—"

"Ivy, that's not—"

"*Listen,*" she said. "I couldn't deal with it. With *you.* On top of everything else." Ivy sighed. "I was too mad. It was like all at once I could see everything piling up. My mom leaving. My dad picking up and moving us here with zero discussion because it was the 'right thing to do.' For him. And then the case. It was your decisions. Your rules."

Ivy plucked at the bedspread, snapping off a thread. "I'm sick and tired of dealing with the fallout from everyone else's choices," she said. Her lips were trembling when she finally looked up. "When do I get to make the rules?"

All of my commands and accusations from the past week came back to punch me in the gut. I'd gone so far off course, it wasn't funny. Pops had hit the nail on the head. Now was the time to dig in and make things right.

"How about now?" I sat down beside Ivy. "I can't do anything about your folks," I said. "But I can change things with us." Ivy's words echoed, and an idea bounced back. "Let's start from scratch. What's our first rule?"

Ivy scratched Spartacus under the chin as she thought. Her jaw was set when she finally spoke. "Rule number one: we help people."

"For a set fee."

"*Howard*," she said. "It's not about money and business or checking and balancing favors. It should be about making a difference. Helping people."

"Yes, okay, fine." I smiled. "We help people. That's good. I know exactly where to start." I filled Ivy in on what I'd learned from the Arts Council and the plan so far.

She grimaced. "That's a terrible plan."

"I know."

"I love it," she said.

-. .. -.-. -.-   .- -. -..   -. --- .-. .-

We made it to Marvin's shop at six on the dot. Ivy and I burst through the door to find Leyla, Carl, and Miles standing in front of the counter.

"Oh, good," I said. "The gang's all here."

"Waiting to hear what for," Leyla said, arms crossed as she glared at me.

Hoarse coughing cut me off as Marvin shuffled out of the back room. "Am I paying you to loiter around my shop?"

"You're not paying me," I said. Stepping over to the door, I locked it and flipped the Open sign. "And you're closed."

Marvin looked at Spartacus, lying on the floor and panting at Ivy's feet. "Is that a dog?"

"Yes?"

Spartacus's tongue lolled out.

"Is it dead?" Marvin took a step back.

"No?" I took a peek at Spartacus. "No, he's fine."

"If it messes on the carpet, you're cleaning it up," he sniffed, and Carl cracked a smile.

"Uncle Marv, a mess would be an improvement on this carpet," Carl said.

Marvin cackled and shuffled back toward his office.

"Good luck storming the castle," he said. "If you get caught, I saw nothing and no one."

"Thanks, Marv," I called after him. Leyla leaned forward, toying with a box of harmonicas on the counter.

"This store is amazing," she said. "It's like a museum of Grantleyville's most bizarre history and collectibles. I could get an article a week out of here."

"One thing at a time," I said. "Let's focus." I brought everyone up to speed and filled Leyla and Carl in on the plan.

"That's a terrible plan," Leyla said.

Miles leaned up against the counter and whistled. "Believe it or not, that's better than the one he told me this afternoon."

Ivy grinned. "I made some improvements."

Miles, Leyla, and Carl nodded, making noises of approval. I knew I should be offended, but we didn't have the time. "Anyway," I said and halted when Leyla held up a hand.

"Your plan needs a little kick," she said. "Remember that lead I was chasing down from Stoverton?"

"Vaguely."

"It paid off." Leyla pulled a folder out of her bag. "Big time." She set it down on the counter and began spreading out newspaper articles and old yearbooks. "I was going to save this for when the deal with you went bust, but I think you actually have a chance of making it work."

We read through the articles and Miles hooted. "Especially with this," he said.

"What do you think?" I looked over at my partner.

"We'll need to tweak the plan a little," Ivy said. "But yeah, I think this'll do. Quite nicely."

"Okay, then," I said, pulling notebooks and pens out of my pockets and passing them around the circle. "Let's get to work."

Chapter Twenty-Eight

On Saturday morning, the five of us stood outside the school, ready for action. Ivy bounced up on the balls of her feet, excitement radiating out through the tips of her toes. "Operation Sportsball is now in effect," she said. Under Ivy's direction, the plan had gone from very terrible to semiterrible.

Miles put his hand up. "Is that—are we really calling it that?"

"Yes," Ivy and I said.

Carl and Miles groaned.

"The name isn't going to make or break the plan," Leyla said, tucking Spartacus under her coat.

"But it helps if it's snazzy," Ivy said. "And we need all the help we can get. Let's get phase one rolling."

"That's Coach's car," Miles said, pointing at the parking lot. If the man of the hour was here, it was time to set things in motion.

"Everybody knows what to do," I said.

Ivy held out a hand. " 'Go, Gladiators' on three?"

Carl and Leyla peeled off to the left and Miles snorted. I fist-bumped her waiting hand and grinned. "Go, Gladiators."

"That's what I'm talking about." Ivy flashed me a smile and headed toward to the school. Miles and I jogged after her.

Rounding the corner to Coach's office, I checked out my partner. "You all set?"

Ivy patted her shirt pocket. "Double and triple checked."

"Okay," I said. "Operation Sportsball is a go."

Miles dipped his head to hide a smirk. "Sure, whatever," he said. "I'll see you guys in a bit."

"I don't think there's anything wrong with a good code name," Ivy said.

"No, no, it works," I said. "I like it."

I held up a finger as we approached Coach's office. Mr. Williams was the picture of desolation, sitting at his desk with his head in his hands. He looked up when we knocked on the cage door, and we took a step back. His eyes were bloodshot and bleary. Coach had had a rough night. He scrambled up from his seat to let us in, scattering papers and knocking his pen cup over. "You got him? Where is he?"

"We ran into a problem," I said as we stepped through the door.

"What do you mean?" Mr. Williams ran a hand through his patchy hair. "What problem? Where is he? Do you not understand how serious this is?"

"We've made some progress," Ivy said. "We know for sure that Carl Dean wasn't involved."

"I don't care about Carl," he snapped. "I care about getting Spartacus back. If we go into the Grudge Game without him and lose, the Parents' Association is going to have my head."

"Don't you want the proper person caught for this?"

"If Carl didn't do this, I can guarantee he did something else. He's as likely a candidate as any, and if people find out about this, I'm going to need someone believable to put the blame on."

"It doesn't matter that he's innocent?" I asked.

"That's a relative concept when it comes to Carl."

"It's one game," Ivy said.

A flush began to creep up Mr. Williams's neck. "One game? *One game?* It's *the* game. I will do whatever it takes for us to win."

"Ah, yes," I said. "You do have some making up to do." I poked through my bag and pulled out the copies of the articles Leyla had dug up. "Ivy, did you know we keep old copies of our school newspaper?"

"I did not, Howard," Ivy said. "Please tell me more."

"It's fascinating stuff, really. A look back at all of our school's triumphs . . . and tragedies."

"Tragedies." Ivy frowned. "What kind of sad memories haunt these hallowed halls?"

I unfolded one of the papers. "Well, this story here is all about the only year we've ever lost the Grudge Game."

A vein began to twitch in Coach's forehead.

"Twenty years ago, it happened. A Grantleyville player accidentally passed to a Stoverton player, allowing them to score the winning points in the final seconds of the game."

"My goodness," Ivy said. "Who would do such a thing?"

"Stop it," Mr. Williams said. "We all know it was me. That game has hounded me my whole life. No one cares how well I played in high school and college. I'm always that guy who lost us the Grudge Game."

"You think winning this year is going to change any of that?" Ivy leaned forward in her chair.

"It has to." Mr. Williams slammed a hand down on his desk. "I've been willing—I've done *everything* for this team." He pushed his chair back to pace his small square of carpet. "Needed money for better uniforms, I stole from other budgets. Bus broke down for our away game, I swiped one from another field trip. Grantleys want their kids to start, I give them first string." Coach shook his head at that. "Most of them are awful, but if their parents donate enough, they're starting."

"Sounds like a lot of effort," I said. "Especially sacrificing other groups for your cause."

"Whatever it takes," he said. "You think anyone actually cares about little Art Club bake sales? No. This town cares about sports. And they never forget." Coach stared off into the distance. "I put blood, sweat, and tears into this team to make up for a two-second mistake. I need a win to change history."

The man was unhinged. I glanced at Ivy as Coach continued his rant unabated. She shrugged. No harm in letting him get it out of his system. I sat back until he started to wind down. "Mr. Williams, I—"

"You bring me that dog by halftime," he said, stabbing a finger in my direction, "or I'm turning you in for investigating on school property."

"For a job you *hired* us to do," Ivy said, jumping out of her seat.

"My word against yours," Mr. Williams snarled. "No one else knows about this little situation. Mrs. Rodriguez thinks you've been following your special guidelines. She'll be shocked to hear otherwise. Get me Spartacus, or we're all going down together. Do you understand?"

Ivy and I stood in stunned silence.

"*Understand?*"

We nodded and backed out of his office. Once we were out of sight, Ivy and I legged it down the hall. I paused for a breather when we reached the safety of the girls' bathroom. Hands on my knees, panting, I looked over at Ivy. "Did you get it?"

She pulled her phone out of her shirt pocket and tapped at the screen. The coach's voice boomed out. "*Understand?*"

Ivy grinned. "Every word."

Chapter Twenty-Nine

Ivy passed her phone off to Leyla and Carl to work their magic, and we grabbed Spartacus to get into position. The gym was filling up fast with people from Grantleyville and Stoverton, elbowing each other to get the best seats. Shades of green and gold butted up against scarlet red as people wore their school pride on their sleeves. Spartacus snuffled from inside my coat. "Hang on, buddy," I said. "We're almost done.

We crept along the back wall and slid under the bleachers. The crowd had filled in enough to cover our position. I peeked through the feet. Players began warming up, filling the air with thuds and squeaks as they moved over the court.

"Oh, no," Ivy said.

"What?"

"I just realized something." She turned to me, despair plain across her face. "We're going to have to actually watch the game."

I knew this plan was terrible.

"No more sports cases after this," I said.

"Agreed."

Spartacus puffed out a breath, and we hunkered down to wait out the rest of Operation Sportsball.

-. .. -.-. -.- .- -. -.. -. --- .-. .-

Half an hour later, music was blaring, signaling the beginning of halftime. The score was tied and tensions were running high. Before anyone could leave, the side door to the gym banged open.

"That's our cue," I said.

Ivy and I walked to the end of the bleachers and took in the scene playing out on the court. Ellis Garcia was striding toward the center of the floor, megaphone in hand. The rest of the Arts Council was lined up behind her, and more kids continued to stream through the door.

Every single kid. From every single arts club.

One after the other they sat down on the floor. Ellis nodded to the stage at the end of the gymnasium. I saw the curtain rustle and then the music cut off.

Leyla and Carl must be in place. Time for phase two.

"We are the Grantleyville Student Arts Council," Ellis shouted into her megaphone. "Today we are protesting the treatment we have received at the hands of Mr. Williams, the Parents' Association, and the school administration."

The crowd began to buzz and stir in their seats.

"Our programs have been cut and taken a backseat to the sports teams. We want our budget back. We want fair use of school space. We want—"

"Get out of here!" someone shouted.

"Yeah, simmer down!" Others started to join in. "Nobody cares."

Ellis faltered, then squared her shoulders. She looked back at her cohorts, nodding and raising a fist in the air. They began to chant as one. "Do your part, save the arts. Do your part, save the arts."

Boos came from all corners, drowning out their message. Mr. Williams stomped over to Ellis and took the megaphone out of her hand.

"Alright, okay," he said, frowning when nothing came out of the speaker. Ellis pointed out the On button and Mr. Williams grumbled, starting again. "Let's settle down."

Leyla's face popped out from behind the curtain on the

stage, and I poked Ivy. She brandished a thumbs-up at Leyla, who disappeared again.

"I know we've got some emotions running high," Mr. Williams said to the crowd. Feedback interrupted him as the speakers came back to life.

"*I don't care about Carl.*" The coach's voice blared through the room. "*I care about getting Spartacus back.*"

"Who's back there?" Mr. Williams shouted toward the stage. I grinned at Ivy. Looked like Carl had successfully managed to break into the AV room.

"*Needed money for better uniforms, I stole from other budgets. Bus broke down for our away game, I swiped one from another field trip. Grantleys want their kids to start, I give them first string.*"

Ellis grabbed the megaphone back. "Our money and our bus. Stolen from the Arts Council field trip."

"*Most of them are awful, but if their parents donate enough, they're starting.*"

Grantley players shook their heads, muttering to each other. Miles stood up and looked at his teammates. "Just like I said, guys." He walked over to stand beside Ellis. Scotty and Oscar followed quickly in his wake along with a good chunk of the rest of the team. They sat as one with the rest of the kids on the floor.

"What are you doing?" Mr. Williams hollered at them.

"*You think anyone actually cares about little Art Club bake sales? No. This town cares about sports. And they never forget.*"

"Turn this off," Mr. Williams screamed at the stage. The noise was rising and blasted up another notch when Jake rose from the bench on his side of the gym. He said a few words to his teammates and was met with some nods and a couple of frowns. Bending low, his face was serious as he kept talking. All of a sudden he turned and walked over to Oscar in the middle of the court. The rest of the Stoverton team followed, and they joined the sit-in on the floor.

"*I need a win to change history.*"

Parents from both towns were shouting at their kids.

"This is going well." We turned to see Leyla and Carl standing behind us. "Time for the finishing touch?" Leyla asked, handing Ivy back her phone.

"Definitely," I said.

"You can do the honors." Leyla held out her phone to Carl, and he pressed the screen.

"*Get me Spartacus, or we're all going down together. Do you understand?*"

Phones started beeping all over the gymnasium. "EXCLUSIVE FROM THE GRANTLEYVILLE MIDDLE SCHOOL BLOG,"

Leyla whispered. "CORRUPTION ON THE COURT – EXPOSING A COACH'S ULTERIOR MOTIVES."

Ivy brought the post up on her phone, and we scrolled through it quickly. "Wow," I said. "That was some fast work, Leyla."

"That's how we do it in the newspaper biz."

Ivy looked out at the crowd poring over their phones. "How many people did this go out to?"

"Everyone with a school email, the Parents' Association, the School Board, local news outlets," she said. Carl poked her, and she trailed off.

I watched as they exchanged a look. "What?"

"Also national news outlets."

"Leyla."

"What? This could be my big break! I'll be a household name." She ran a hand through the air. "Leyla Bashir, investigative reporter."

The volume from the gym was increasing as people read through Leyla's article. She'd dragged everything out into the open. The cuts to the arts programs, the coach's dirty dealings and past failures, the kidnapping of Spartacus, Carl's innocence. It was all laid out with a few key names missing: Howard Wallace and Ivy Mason. After all, we weren't supposed to be investigating on school grounds. Ivy and I thought it was best to let Leyla take the credit.

Leyla agreed.

"I want everyone to *be quiet!*" shouted Mrs. Rodriguez, standing in the middle of the gym, one hand on her hip, the other holding the megaphone. She spotted the group of us standing beside the bleachers and exhaled slowly. "Why am I not surprised?" she said, rubbing her eyes.

"I want—" Mr. Williams started.

"You want to stay right there and shush," Mrs. Rodriguez said to him. She faced the crowd. "The Grudge Game is always an exciting day, but I think this has raised the bar."

The room finally quieted down and she continued. "The information brought forth today is shocking and requires some serious discussion. Rest assured that action will be taken." She put down the megaphone and spoke with Ellis for a few minutes. Ellis nodded solemnly and motioned to the kids on the floor.

"What is this?" Mr. Williams paced in front of the benches. "Are you letting them get away with this? With that article? It's straight libel!"

A group of well-dressed adults walked over to him, and his face went gray.

"That's the school board," Leyla said.

We watched from our post as the board members walked Mr. Williams out of the gym. He spotted us and glared. I waved at him with Spartacus's paw. Next came Mrs. Rodriguez and Ellis. "Leyla," Mrs. Rodriguez said, "come for a chat."

"Freedom of the press," Leyla blurted out.

Mrs. Rodriguez sighed. "Ms. Bashir, it's simply a chat."

Leyla fell into step beside Ellis, giving her a friendly hip bump. We watched as they headed out the door. Carl held out his hands, and I passed him Spartacus. "Go, team," I said.

He jogged over to the bench where the rest of the Gladiators were milling around. They shouted when they saw Carl with Spartacus in his arms. Soon the little dog was surrounded by pats and belly rubs.

"Are we here to gawk, or are we gonna play some ball?" Ms. Kowalski stood by the bench, clutching a clipboard and wearing a whistle around her neck.

"Um, Ms. Kowalski?" Oscar stepped over to her. "Should you be—"

"Played all though school," she barked. "Coach three rec league teams. Think I can handle it." She blew a fierce note out on the whistle. "Come on. We've got a game to win."

Miles spotted us lingering, and he jogged over. "You going to stay and watch?"

Ivy and I looked at each other, weighing the options.

"Come on," Miles said. "You've got to see Operation Sportsball to the end."

My partner gasped. "I knew it would catch on."

"I guess we can stay," I said, "for a bit."

Chapter Thirty

Ivy and I sat in the garage office, relaxing in the aftermath of a job well done. My partner scrolled through her phone. "Three more outlets have picked up Leyla's story," she said.

"She's going to be unbearable now," I said.

"She's earned it." Ivy grinned. "We couldn't have pulled it off without her—or Carl."

"What else does it say in there?" I nodded at her phone.

"Mr. Williams is under review. Suspended until further notice."

"Good." We'd heard from Marvin that Carl was back on the team. He said we were officially square now. Ellis, Ashi, Scotty, and the rest of the Arts Council were serving detention for their role in the dognapping, but they didn't mind. The clubs were finally getting their field trip. Even better, after a number of editorials discussing the need for arts in schools, the Parents' Association was spearheading new fundraising efforts for their programs. We'd survived watching a whole basketball game and, oddly enough, the Grudge Game had ended in a tie. After the dramatic events of the day, battling it out in overtime didn't sit right. Both teams were happy to walk away on a handshake. Until next year anyway.

All in all, a job well done.

I looked over at Ivy, hanging out in the stinky, comfy chair, patting Blue's handlebars. "Good work, partner."

She grinned at me. "You, too."

"Things got kind of hairy for a while there," I said, nodding at her bag leaning up against the chair. "We never finished talking about that."

Ivy pulled her bag up off the floor and fished out the rumpled white envelope. "I don't know what else to say about it," she said, worrying one corner after another. "And I definitely don't know what to do."

"I have an idea," I said. Walking over to the filing cabinet, I opened the top drawer where we kept our open cases. "File it."

"What?"

"File it," I said. "We'll deal with it when you're ready."

Ivy hopped up and peered into the drawer. "*M* for Mason?"

"Why start worrying about proper alphabetizing now?"

"Good point," she said. "*P* for Pending Parental Problems." She stuffed the envelope in the drawer and slid it shut. Ivy sighed and looked at me. "Thanks, Howard."

I reached out to pat her shoulder and she grabbed me, pulling me in for a hug. "We're partners, Ivy. That's what we do." What I should have been doing all along. I squeezed her back.

The garage shook as someone banged on the door. "Alright, relax," I shouted, "I'm coming." I opened the door to see not only the last person I expected, but five others.

"Hi," said Miles.

"We're going to the bakery," said Ellis.

"To celebrate the fact that I'm famous," Leyla said, grinning. Carl nodded.

"You guys should come," Scotty added, and Ashi popped out from behind him. "Please?"

Ivy stood beside me in the doorway. She stayed quiet, leaving the decision up to me. My chest tightened as I stared at the crew before us. Staying in would be easy. Ivy looked at me and smiled a little. Going out would be interesting.

"Will there be hot chocolate?"

"It's Mrs. Hernandez," Ellis said. "There'll be at least six kinds."

"Let's go," I said, slapping on my hat and tossing my partner hers. Locking the door behind us, Ivy and I stepped out to join the group. As we made our way down to the sidewalk Leyla started talking about her Pulitzer acceptance speech while Ashi listened with wide eyes. Ellis and Ivy were chatting about the upcoming musical, and Carl and Scotty discussed new plays for the team.

Miles fell into step beside me. "This is kind of weird," he said. I murmured in agreement. "But not bad weird?" He searched my face, trying to gauge a reply before I answered.

"No," I said, watching everyone laugh and talk. "Not bad weird."

"Where'd you get that hat?" He tipped a finger at his own forehead.

"This?' Ivy swung back to sling an arm over my shoulder. She tapped at the brim of her own hat. "This you gotta earn."

"Fair enough," Miles said, hiding his smile. He caught up with Carl and Scotty to talk more shop.

I looked at my partner. "Don't say it. Don't even say it."

"Bigger sticky notes, friend," she said, looking out at the crowd in front of us. "We're going to need bigger sticky notes."

Wallace and Mason Investigations

~~Mason and Wallace Investigations~~

Rules of Private Investigation

THE GOLDEN RULE: WE HELP PEOPLE.

1. Work with what you've got. Especially when it's a fabulous shade of green.
2. Ask the right questions.
3. Know your surroundings.
4. Always have a cover story ready.
5. Blend in.
6. A bad plan is better than no plan. I think we need to revisit this rule. No.
7. Never underestimate your opponent.
8. Never tip your hand.
9. Don't get caught. You should try following this rule, Howard. Stop it.
10. Pick your battles.
11. Don't leave a trail.
12. Everyone has a hook.
13. Always listen to your partner. She's a genius. Speaking of rules we need to revisit. Very funny.
14. No more sports cases. (AGREED.)

Acknowledgments

To Molly Ker Hawn, thank you for continuing to be the most amazing agent in the world. I am eternally grateful for your hard work and well-timed jokes.

To Christina Pulles, editor extraordinaire, thank you for always asking the right questions. You helped turn these words into the story I hoped it could be.

Thank you to the amazing Sterling family: Hanna Otero, Theresa Thompson, Scott Amerman, Brian Phair, Terence Campo, Heather Kelly, Irene Vandervoort, Sari Lampert Murray, Ardi Alspach, Chris Vaccari, Maha Khalil, and the rest of the fantastic sales team.

To Larissa Gaudet and the Canadian Manda Group, thank you for being an awesome North-side squad.

Thank you to Brian and Winnie Gare for providing me with a much-needed writing sanctuary.

I'm so honored to benefit from the magical critique partner stylings of Naomi Hughes, Kendra Young, Wendy Parris, Laura Shovan, Margaret Dilloway, and Karina Glaser. Thank you, friends!

Thank you to the fantastic Sweet Sixteens and Kick-Butt Kidlit for all the cheers and group hugs.

To Jean Moir and my friends and coworkers at the Middlesex County Library, thank you for all of your wonderful support and for giving me the time to make this book a reality.

Thank you to all of my friends and family who have showered me in enthusiasm and encouragement. Especially my sisters, Jordan and Aidan, who are the best at late night chats and cheers.

To Mom and Dad, the actual best parents in the world, I wish I had a bigger word than thank you. You are both amazing and this adventure wouldn't be happening without you.

And finally, to all the readers who have embraced Howard and Ivy, thank you so much! I'm thrilled to be sharing this dream come true with you.

Turn the page for a sneak peek at the next book featuring Howard and Ivy:

HOWARD WALLACE, P.I.

SABOTAGE STAGE LEFT

Chapter One

"Sure that's the guy?"

The voice stretched across the hall over the hustle and bustle of lunchtime traffic. I bit back a laugh at the incredulous tone, steadying myself against the flow of bodies bumping by. End of the week, everyone got a bit clumsier, a little more careless. As I grabbed my bag out of my locker, I heard the scoffing reply:

"You see anybody else walking around in a bathrobe?"

Lucky coat. I tugged down a brown terrycloth sleeve. Big difference.

My partner bopped up to stand beside me. "Is that our twelve o'clock I see lurking over there?" Ivy rolled up on her tiptoes to peer over my shoulder. "They look twitchy."

"Waiting's good," I said. "Builds character."

"What?" Ivy slid me a sideways look. "Are we billing by the hour now?"

I snorted when she towed me down the hall, stepping up to the two waiting girls. They leapt to attention, one with an eager smile and the other keeping a wary eye.

"Caitlyn." Nodding at our client, I turned my attention to her watchful tagalong. "Didn't realize we'd have company. Who's your friend?"

The tiny, blond sixth grader flicked an impatient wave back at me. "This is Denice. She heard you were helping me and invited herself along." She rolled her eyes. "She said I shouldn't be meeting you by myself."

I could respect a healthy level of suspicion. "Nothing wrong with a little backup," I said. "Shall we take this into my office?" Holding open the door, I waited as Ivy and Caitlyn stepped inside. Denice leaned past me to look in, hovering at the threshold. "Well?" I waved her on.

"This is the girls' bathroom," she said, wrinkling her nose.

"I spend my time solving cases, not scoping out real estate. Be happy it's not the boys'." I walked into the room, letting the door swing shut behind me. It opened a crack as Denice scooted in and hurried over to Caitlyn's side.

"Why did you hire this guy?" She muttered down to Caitlyn, worrying the end of her braid with her fingers. "He's cranky."

"Because he gets results," I said, reaching into my pocket. I pulled out a USB stick and held it out to our client.

Caitlyn let out a shriek as she grabbed the stick from my hand. "You found it? Oh, my gosh. Thank you." She clutched it to her chest, eyes watering. "I was so worried. I thought it was lost forever. How did you find it?"

"Good old-fashioned legwork." Ivy boosted herself up on one of the sinks. "Got the schedule for the computer lab, made some inquiries, twisted a few arms. The usual." She swung her feet back and forth, hands braced behind her on the sides of the sink. "What's on that thing that's so important, anyway?"

I shot a look at my partner. Knowing our client's business was a world away from asking our client's business. Ivy shrugged, casually ignoring the confines of professional nosiness.

"Oh." Caitlyn blushed faintly. "It's my novel," she said. "I've been working on it since last year."

"Quite the treasure to leave lying around," I said. People let the small size of Grantleyville lull them into a false sense of security. Their vulnerability made for our gain, but cases like Caitlyn's didn't always have a happy ending. "Should look at expanding your backup into digital."

Denice nodded sagely, a faint note of approval flashing behind her black-framed glasses. She pushed them up the bridge of her nose with a spindly finger. "That's what I keep telling her."

"I've got backup out the wazoo," Caitlyn said, dismissing our concerns with a shake of her head. "This is one of a billion copies. I was just worried about it getting lost and falling into the wrong hands. It's not ready for the world to read yet." She kissed the USB before stuffing it deep into her bag and stepped back to give me a beaming smile. "Ally was right about you."

Ivy perked up in her seat. "How so?"

"She said you were the ones who could help me," she said. "That you know your stuff. And she was so right!" Caitlyn threw herself forward, grabbing me in a viselike grip. "Thank you so, so much!"

I blinked at my partner who shook with silent laughter while I endured the crushing hug. "We aim to please," I said. "Now there is the small matter of your bill."

"Oh, yeah!" Caitlyn released her octopus hold and dug

through her pockets. "Here you go," she said, thrusting a crumpled envelope into my hands.

"How much did they charge you?" Denice asked under her breath.

"Not enough," Caitlyn said. "Seriously, I would have paid way more to get it back. You guys are worth every penny. Do you have more of those sticky notes? I want to give them to my friends."

"Business cards," I corrected, dragging a stack out from the depths of my coat. I pulled a few off the top and handed them over. "Glad we could be of service."

Denice dragged her friend out the door as Caitlyn continued to call out her thanks. Huffing out a breath, I set about straightening my hug-rumpled attire.

"Another happy customer," Ivy said cheerfully. "And it sounds like we should think about upping our rates." She tapped a finger against her lips. "Who's Ally?"

I racked my brain. "No clue."

"Word must be getting around." Ivy rubbed her hands together, cackling.

A toilet flushed, and we both froze. I whipped around to glare at my partner.

"You didn't check the stalls," I said.

"You were supposed to check them," Ivy shot back.

"I was talking to our client," I said, one eye on the stall door swinging open. A tall girl emerged, hitching her bag over one shoulder. She walked up to the sink, studiously ignoring us, and began washing her hands.

"Hi." Ivy said, leaning over from her perch on the neighboring sink. "Wallace and Mason Investigations. How's it going?"

The girl shook out her hands and scooted around Ivy to the paper towel dispenser. We stood in silence, listening to the roll crunch forward as she pulled out three pieces in quick succession.

"I swear we're very organized and efficient," Ivy continued. "Here for all of your investigative needs."

That earned Ivy an eyebrow-raise as the girl chucked her paper towels in the garbage. It sailed in with a light swish, and I handed her one of our cards before she headed out the door.

"Tell your friends," Ivy said to her retreating back.

"Smooth." I dragged a hand over my face as the door closed. "Stall checks, Ivy," I said.

"That was super smooth!" Ivy hopped off the sink to waggle a finger at me. "And yes, I missed the stall checks, but maybe we got a new client out of it? More importantly, we still haven't figured out who Ally is."

"Word must be getting around," I said. "People have heard about the agency and the cases we've solved."

"What I'm hearing is that we have fans." Ivy did a little dance stopping abruptly midmove to stare at me.

I took a step back. "What?"

She leaned in, narrowing her gaze into a squint. "There's something wrong with your face. Your cheeks are all squished up." She pinched at her own. "And I can see your teeth? It's weird. I think we should go see the nurse."

"Shut up." I ran a hand over my mouth, but it was no help against the smile stretching it from side to side. "I'm not used to attention without violence attached to it. Or detention. Let me enjoy the moment."

"Yes," Ivy said, diving into her bag to rummage around for her lunch. "Enjoy it, my friend." She raised her water bottle. "Cheers to Ally. May she continue to provide us with free advertising—whoever she is."

I tipped my drink against hers, and we settled down onto the floor to eat our lunch. Stuffing my returning grin full of sandwich, I fully enjoyed the moment. I'd been at the detective thing for close to a year now. Ivy'd been on board since the fall, and we'd slowly but surely put a team together. We'd worked a few major cases so I wasn't completely surprised how far news had spread, but I couldn't deny it was nice to have people uttering my name with a positive ring for a change. Felt like a step in the right direction.

If only that step wasn't trailing toilet paper.

"I miss having a proper office," I said, glancing around at the paint peeling off the walls and the water-spotted ceiling.

Ivy's head snapped up at that. "You miss having a broken-down desk held up by pickle buckets? Outside in the open elements? Left vulnerable to squirrel attacks?"

"When you put it like that," I said. "Yes. Yes, I do." I flapped a hand at the dripping sinks and gurgling toilets. "It's not like we're currently putting our best foot forward. I miss having our own space. We need better digs."

"Hard to find better digs when we're not supposed to be investigating on school property in the first place," Ivy said. "It's called keeping a low profile."

Being banned from conducting any at-school investigations put a major cramp in our activities. That rule was laid down months ago. Now that they'd had some time to cool off, I felt fairly certain that the administration would agree with my 'what they don't see won't enrage them' policy. Hence the bathroom base of operations.

"Like anyone's paying attention to what we're doing these days," I said. "It's spring musical city out there, and we're sliding right under the radar."

Ivy made a noise of agreement as she chewed her cookie.

"You still doing okay with all of that?" I asked. "Doing this stuff and the musical? We'll survive if you need to take more of a break."

Ivy joined the Grantleyville Middle School Drama Club as part of a cover story for an investigation a few months back. The case was long closed, but she'd enjoyed the group enough to stick around. Why was a mystery I had yet to solve. The club was putting on *Little Shop of Horrors* for the spring musical and Ivy was helping both on stage and off. With only two weeks left to showtime, it was all hands on deck.

"This was probably my last job for the next couple weeks," Ivy admitted. "We're going to have more rehearsals leading up to opening night and Mrs. Pamuk doesn't want anyone missing one if we can help it."

"Makes sense," I said. "I pushed our meeting back so I can still help out after school."

Ivy choked a bit on her cookie, and I patted her on the back. "That's okay," she croaked out, brushing a chunk of curly brown hair out of her face. "You don't have to come by. I know you're busy."

"I'm not going to leave my partner in the lurch." I grinned at Ivy. "I can spare an hour to do some grunt work."

"Yeah," Ivy said. "Yes, for sure. You should definitely come help. That would be great."

That was about three confirmations too many. Ivy was cast in the musical back in February, and I'd recently started to help out as the behind-the-scenes action picked up. I thought things had been running smoothly up until now.

"Or not," I said. "I can hang around until you're done." Never let it be said Howard Wallace can't take a hint.

"No," Ivy said. "I want you there. It's—some of the crew members were underappreciative of your handiwork from last time."

"Everything went great!"

"Howard, you nailed your pants to the backdrop," she said, ignoring my attempts to wave her off. "While you were wearing them."

"That's fine," I said with a shrug. "I don't have to work on the construction side. I can paint."

Ivy caught her flinch before her shoulders followed through.

"What." Toddlers can paint. What possible complaint could there be about my painting skills?

"I just—" She let out a little high-pitched hum. "I mean, you remember what the home office looks like, right?"

Built by Pops and myself. Not a masterpiece by most standards, but serviceable. In the right wind conditions.

"That was artistic license," I said. "Those gaps are for aesthetic purposes only. It only dried like that because they mixed it wrong. I can paint. I'll follow the instructions. It'll be *fine*."

ABOUT THE AUTHOR

CASEY LYALL (5'4", brown hair, blue eyes, no known aliases) is a middle grade writer from southwestern Ontario, and the author of *Howard Wallace, P.I.* She works at her local library, where she runs a number of writing groups for kids. When she's not writing, Casey loves to bake, watch an "unhealthy" amount of movies and television, and of course, read. She'd consider adding detective work to the list if she could find a proper coat. You can find her on Twitter as @CKLyall and at caseylyall.com.